Sir Licksalot
&
The Island Fools

Written by D.L. Carroll
Illustrated by Teri Cuneo

PublishAmerica
Baltimore

Softcover 9781462680924
PUBLISHED BY PUBLISHAMERICA, LLLP
www.publishamerica.com
Baltimore

Printed in the United States of America

Ashley!
Aloha My Friend!,

D. L. Carroll

"For the adventurer"

Acknowledgement

Special thanks to my friend, Randon Roman for the native translations.

CHAPTER 1
The Secret

Staring at our big secret, we wolf down our lunch. No one is talking. The only sounds we hear are that of potato chips being crunched, and water splashing in the fountain. Sir Licksalot wanders up to us wagging his fluffy tail. I look at him and ask, "What do you want boy?"

Sir Licksalot sits up on his hind legs with his front paws dangling down his chest with his mouth slightly open, appearing as though he is grinning.

"He wants some lunch too," Danny answers. Looking at Sir Licksalot he teases him. "You want some hot dog?"

Sir Licksalot's eyes get really big, and his skinny pink tongue hangs down.

Making a motion with his hand as if he is throwing something, Bobby tells Sir Licksalot to go and get his bone.

Sir Licksalot doesn't budge.

Timmy laughs. "He is smarter than you Bobby."

"Whatever. I thought all dogs like to fetch," Bobby responds.

"Not when they can smell people food," Cici explains. "Why don't you give him some of yours Timmy? You've already had two hot dogs and a cheeseburger."

"No way! I earned this lunch," Timmy says, wiping his brow.

"As if the rest of us didn't get chased by sharks, dropped from a seven story cliff, and sucked under by a rip tide? You weren't alone on the adventure into Mavericks Extreme Water Cave," Danny reminds him.

"Yeah!" Cici mumbles. "Going on the adventure in the magic fountain is the greatest fun I have ever had!"

The other girls nod in agreement as they continue chewing.

"The best part was that no one, not even our parents, knew we were gone because time stops when you go on the adventure," Danny adds.

Looking right at me, Cici inquires, "Do you think we can do it again?"

Not really knowing the answer, I shrug my shoulders. "I guess. I don't see why not. Have you ever heard of this happening to anyone that lived at this house before we moved in?"

"No," Cici answers. "Have you guys?"

"Can't say that I have," Danny says.

"Do you think the magic fountain will take us right back to the cave?" Jesse asks, wiping her mouth as she finishes the last bite of her barbequed cheeseburger.

"With our dumb luck, we will end up back in the middle of the ocean with the sharks. No, thank you!" Bobby exclaims.

"Seriously dude, wouldn't it be fun to go back? Are you saying you wouldn't want to go?" Timmy asks.

Bobby turns to Timmy. "You just want to go to the land of plenty, where they have plenty of food, plenty of music, and plenty of girls."

"And what's wrong with that?" Timmy asks, grinning.

"Nothing if you want to look like a porker. Wouldn't you rather be hot like me?" Bobby says lifting his shirt up and pushing his chest out, rubbing his six pack.

I just can't help myself. "Who would want to be a Hecka Old Turd?" I mumble.

Everyone starts laughing.

"Good one Blaze," Cici mumbles.

"Oh thanks little sis, I can see where your loyalty lies," Bobby says, pulling his shirt down in embarrassment as he starts to walk towards the house.

"Wait Bobby, I was just kidding. What? You can dish it out, but you can't take it!" I yell after him.

"I thought we had a deal in Mavericks that I wouldn't call anyone names, and you wouldn't tell my secrets," Bobby reminds me.

"Uh, duh, you called Timmy a porker," Cici states, with her hands on her hips.

Bobby points to Timmy. "Well, look at him, he is hauling around a spare tire. It wasn't a name, it's the truth."

Timmy gets a frown on his face. "Well, at least everyone likes to hang out with me. I can't say that about you, Bobby."

"Whatever. I'm outta here," Bobby says. "I'm leaving. Are you coming or not?" he asks Cici.

Cici, feeling as if she has to go along with her brother says, "Bye, Blaze. Thanks for the adventure. It was an adventure I will never forget."

I give Cici a nod in acknowledgment.

Danny looks at his sister, Jesse, and says, "I'm tired too. We should probably leave."

Timmy and his little sister Tabitha are still sitting by the magic fountain with me and Sir Licksalot. Tabitha strokes Sir Licksalot's head, and Timmy stares into the fountain dreamily, humming under his breath.

"What do you think dude? Do you think magic can happen twice? Do you think we can go back?" Timmy asks me.

"Heck, yeah!" I exclaim, though of course I am not really sure. "I'm not wasting my summer vacation because big bad Bobby is afraid of sharks. I'm in for going again."

"Me too," Timmy says. "How about next weekend?"

I instantly respond, "Sounds good to me. I will check to see if my parents have any plans for us to make sure I'll be home. I'll let you know."

Tabitha, Timmy, and I get up and walk to the back door of the house. Sir Licksalot runs in front of us to get in first, collecting his Dingo bone along the way.

Inside the house, the adults are helping my mom and dad clean up from the barbeque. The men are folding up and putting away the tables and chairs. The ladies are wrapping up the leftover food placing both the drinks and food in the refrigerator.

"Did you kids have a good time Blaze?" Mom asks, smiling at me.

"Uh yeah, it was alright I guess," I say, not wanting to seem overly eager. I don't want to accidentally slip up and give away our secret.

"Good. Now go help your dad get the rest of the stuff in the yard picked up and put away. After you finish helping your dad, please take Sir Licksalot for his walk."

"Do I have to?"

Mom gives me the glare, and I know right then and there that I better do as she says and quickly.

After Dad and I finally finish putting everything away, I go into my room to grab my iPod and my ear buds. Stuffing them into my pockets I walk into the kitchen to grab Sir Licksalot's leash and poop bag. Sir Licksalot hears the rustling plastic bags and he races into the kitchen, sliding across the floor like a dust mop. I put his leash on him and then stick my ear buds in my ears. I find my favorite song on the iPod, "Gotta Feeling," by the Black Eyed Peas and head out the door to take Sir Licksalot for a walk.

CHAPTER 2
Middle School

By the time Sir Licksalot and I get home, the house is all cleaned up and the neighbors are gone. My mom is taking a shower and my dad is watching T.V. I take Sir Licksalot's leash off and go out into the backyard to toss his incredibly stinky poop bag away into the trashcan. Walking back in through the door, I ask my dad, "Do we have any plans next weekend?"

"Not that I am aware of. Why?" Dad replies.

"No reason, just wondering. I'm going to go play Battlefield on my XBOX."

"When your mom gets out of the shower she has a surprise for you."

"Really! What?"

"I can't tell you. It will ruin her surprise," Dad says with a cheerful grin.

Not long after, the running water from the shower stops. I walk quickly down the hall towards the bathroom. "Mom, Dad said you have a surprise for me. What is it?"

"Hold on Blaze. Let me get out of the shower and get dressed first," Mom shouts through the bathroom door. I can tell from her voice that she is smiling. What is she up to?

Sitting on the edge of my parents bed, I begin tapping my fingers on the night stand. Sir Licksalot crawls out from under the bed, doing his version of the slow army crawl. I pick him up and place him on my lap. "What do you think it is boy?"

Sir Licksalot wags his tail and licks me on the face.

"I sure hope she will say that I am going to see my old friends from the city. Moving here to the beach front has its pros, but also its cons. I miss my old friends so much."

Mom enters into the room. "I'm sorry, Blaze, they are still at camp. I told you they will be there all summer long."

"I thought you made friends with the neighborhood kids during our barbeque," Mom says with a look of concern on her face. "That is why we gave the party, so that you could make some new friends."

"They are okay, I guess. Cici is kinda bossy and she is such a smart aleck. She thinks she is the center of the universe, just like all dumb blondes"

"Don't stereotype, Blaze. Cici is a pretty smart girl for a nine-year old," Mom says as if she knows Cici well. "Is she starting fourth grade or fifth grade in the fall?"

"She will be a fifth grader. Just like Timmy. Timmy is eleven though. Why are people of such different ages in the same grade?"

"It depends on when your birthday is. The schools use a calendar with a birthday cutoff for entry into kindergarten. You are one of the youngest going into sixth grade because you just turned eleven. Timmy's birthday must be later in the year, which means he missed the cutoff and started kindergarten a year later, at age six. You started kindergarten at age five. Does that make sense?"

"Yeah, I guess."

"Cici must have a birthday coming up soon, most likely before school starts," Mom quickly calculates in her head. Then she asks, "Which one is Timmy?"

"He is the one who likes to eat a lot," I say with a snicker.

"Ah the cute little boy that likes music, correct?" Mom says as she tries to recollect who Timmy is.

"Well, I wouldn't say that he is little."

Mom looks at me frowning. "Don't be rude Blaze. Everyone is built differently."

"Bobby thinks he is 'built.' He thinks that seventh and eighth graders will be afraid of him because he is so strong."

"Oh. Is he the older boy with the attitude?" Mom asks.

"He isn't that much older. He will turn twelve around Christmas. He's mean and calls us all names and seems really tough, but I get the feeling he isn't very happy."

"Hmm," Mom says.

"I think Bobby and Cici are unhappy because they miss their dad."

"It is so sad that they lost their dad at such an early age. I really like their mom. They appear to be good kids from what she told me about them."

Not wanting to argue with my mom, I decide to agree with her, "If you say so."

"Who is the kid who always has a skateboard and who carries gadgets around?" Mom asks.

"That is Danny. I think I like him the best. He is incredibly smart, he gets my sense of humor, and he is only a couple of months older than me. He can be a little weird and geeky, but I don't care because we all have something weird about us, right?"

Mom grabs my chin and looks me in the eye, "Yes, Blaze, we all bring something different into this world. That's what makes each of us unique and special. You have to accept people for their good qualities and their quirks too. Human beings are not perfect, and everyone has a different and unique purpose."

Rolling my eyes I ask, "Are we done talking now?"

Mom smiles and says, "Does my son want his surprise?"

"Yeah, I didn't sit through this sappy talk for nothing!"

"Hey!"

"Kidding Mom. Just kidding!"

"Dad and I were talking and we thought that since you will be going to middle school in the fall it would be a good time to buy you a cell phone. I want you to call me when you get to school and when you get home so that I know that you are safe. The middle school is a couple of miles away so you will be riding your bike this coming year."

"No way. Really? Seriously? You are going to get me a phone?"

"Yes, and we will let you pick it out," Mom says with a twinkle in her eyes.

"Awesome! When can we get it? Can we go now?"

"We will go in the morning, after church."

Rubbing Sir Licksalot's belly I look down and tell him, "Sick! I'm going to have my own phone. I will be able to text my friends."

Then I remember that I don't have that many friends anymore. I only have Timmy and Danny. I kinda think Danny's sister, Jesse, and Timmy's sister, Tabitha, like me, but the other two, Cici and Bobby, they are hard to read. One minute they seem to hate me, and the next minute they like me. Maybe when I start middle school I will meet more people like me: kids who are athletic, stylish and witty. Until then, I hope at least Danny will continue to like me even after the thrill of our adventure in Mavericks fades.

CHAPTER 3
The Phone

The bright summer sun shines straight through my bedroom window. Sir Licksalot is wiggling out from under the covers as I move the covers over my head to cover my eyes from the light. He stretches to reach up to my face and gives me a gigantic good morning slobbery kiss.

"Oh my gosh! Get away from me, you smell like you ate poop!"

Sir Licksalot keeps licking me.

"Dude, you stink, go find your bone," I tell him, pulling the covers tight around my head to block him.

Sir Licksalot starts whining.

"Oh come on! Now? Are you kidding me?"

Sir Licksalot starts barking and jumping around on my bed.

"What is your problem?"

Sir Licksalot lays his head down between his paws and stares at me with sad puppy eyes.

"Okay, Okay. Let's go outside," I say, lowering Sir Licksalot down to the floor.

Sir Licksalot makes a mad dash for the back door, losing traction at every stride because his long hair has grown over his paw pads. His legs slide out to the side of him and he goes sliding into the door head first.

"Oh, you are a smart one!" I say, laughing as I open the door. "Go pee."

Sir Licksalot starts barking. "Dude, be quiet, you are going to wake everyone up."

I walk out towards the fountain and Sir Licksalot jumps up on the rim of the fountain and looks in.

"Oh no. We are not going anywhere today. I get my phone today," I comment pulling Sir Licksalot down from the fountain. "Go pee already."

Sir Licksalot relieves himself and then runs back into the house. He finds his Dingo bone and lies on his bed chewing on it. I stumble my way into the bathroom. When I see myself in the mirror I can't help smiling. What a sight! My hair is plastered to one side of my face, and on the other side, my hair is sticking straight up in the air.

Eager to get started with my day (and to get my own cell phone), I decide to get ready. I turn the shower on and get in. Ten minutes later, I turn the shower off and I remember that I forgot to get a towel. Sneaking around the bathroom door, I look to see if anyone is awake. Only Sir Licksalot is awake and he is sitting right under my nose. I quickly run out of the bathroom to grab a towel from the linen closet. Sir Licksalot sneaks into the bathroom. I race back into the steamy and warm bathroom and begin to dry off. I dry off the upper half of my body and wrap the towel around my waist. Sir Licksalot starts licking the water off my feet and my legs.

"Dude, gross. Stop that!" I tell him, trying to shoo him away.

I reach into the medicine cabinet to get my toothbrush and toothpaste so I can brush my teeth. Sir Licksalot sneaks back over to me and with a playful growl he quickly grabs the corner of my towel and yanks in it as hard as he can. My towel starts to fall off, I lose my balance trying to grab it, and wind up falling on the floor right on my rump. Sir Licksalot is excited and jumps on top of me licking me to death. I start laughing really loudly and my mom comes down the hallway to see what the ruckus is all about.

"Everything okay, Blaze?"

Still giggling I manage to call out to her. "Yeah mom, just playing with Sir Licksalot."

"I'm amazed that you are up already. You aren't usually so excited to go to church," she teased.

"Sir Licksalot woke me up and then I remembered that I am going to get my phone today. I want to have time to go online before church and compare the phones I want to get. This way I will know what I want when we get to the store."

"Now that is called using your head, son."

"My mom didn't raise a fool."

"I heard the kids say something yesterday at the barbeque about being 'The Fools.' What is that all about?" Mom asks.

Trying to figure out how to keep our secret, I stumble on my words, "Huh, What did you say?"

I said, "Why do the kids call themselves, The Fools?"

"It means Friends Outside Our Local Surf."

"That sounds like something you would come up with, Blaze. Maybe they are more like you than you think?"

"I guess," I say, not wanting to continue this discussion. "I need to get dressed. I'm cold," I call out.

"Okay. Come to the kitchen table in thirty minutes for breakfast."

"No problem."

Mom heads towards the kitchen to make breakfast, and I walk towards my bedroom. I turn the computer on and get dressed while it boots up. Sitting down at my desk, I begin my search.

Searching every possible website advertising cell phones, I find the ultimate phone. Excited and smiling from ear to ear, I walk into the kitchen and sit down for breakfast.

Dad looks at me. "You look like the cat that ate the canary. What do you have up your sleeve?"

"Nothing. Nothing at all. It's just a great day."

"Why don't I believe you?" Dad questions me with a cynical look.

"I found the phone I want to get today."

"Ah, that explains it. How much?"

"Its only two hundred and fifty dollars," I say with pleading eyes.

"Only?" Dad says raising his eyebrows.

"The other phones I want are like four hundred dollars."

"That is just insane. I can buy new tires for the truck for four hundred dollars!" Dad says shaking his head. "Let's see what the store offers. Maybe they will have a sale or promotion that we can capitalize on."

"But dad, I really want this one. I will be the coolest kid in the neighborhood."

Mom makes a noise that tells me to stop while I am still ahead.

We finish eating our breakfast and Mom gives Sir Licksalot the leftovers before she shoos him into the backyard. We gather our stuff and leave for church.

After church, we drive to the store to get my new phone. As we drive, Mom brings up the one topic of conversation that I have been avoiding.

"Are you excited to start middle school?" Mom asks.

"Not really."

"Why not?"

"Because it sucked moving here for the end of fifth grade, and now middle school is going to be even worse. I didn't fit in then, and I am not going to fit in now."

"What are you talking about Blaze? Everyone wants to be your friend."

"Not."

"You have friends, stop acting like you don't," Dad says, sounding annoyed.

"But they are not like Cody and Logan. No one is ever going to take their place, and I will never be that popular again. It is like I am an outcast. They all seem to think that I talk weird and look weird. I'm different from everyone here, so why would anyone want to be my friend?"

"Blaze, you are being ridiculous and over dramatic," Mom says, though she really doesn't get it.

"Perhaps we should enroll you in drama classes," Dad says laughing.

"Funny. You don't understand. Middle school is different. You have to make it to every class on time, and the school campus is so big. Everyone needs to belong to a group. If you don't, then you are a loner, or a nerd, and people pick on you or want to beat you up. If they don't want to beat you up, then they want you to smoke or do drugs with them. Explain to me what is so great about starting middle school."

"You have a group. Bobby and Danny will transition to the new school with you. Just stick with them and together you can support each other and everything will be fine," Mom says in her nurturing voice.

"Yeah, that is if they still want to be my friends when we go to school after summer break."

"I missed that, what did you say Blaze?"

"Nothing," I mumble. "Turn here Dad. The store is right there, next to Starbucks."

"I will run in and get us some coffee, while you two get the phone," Mom tells Dad.

Walking into the Verizon store, I am feeling very confident that Dad will get me the phone I want. I walk right over to the counter and ask to see the iPhone. The sales clerk pulls the phone out from under the counter and he lets me test it.

"Dad, I want it. Can I please get it?" I ask.

"Let's have a look at some of these other phones that aren't as expensive," Dad says.

Despite my attempts to negotiate, my begging, and my pleading, Dad wins. I don't get the phone I want, but I do get a phone that is pretty sick. The phone has a touch screen, and underneath there is a keyboard. I will be able to hold the phone in my lap and text without the teacher seeing what I am doing.

Driving back into our neighborhood, I see Bobby, Timmy, and Danny riding their skateboards. Dad slows down so that he doesn't hit them.

I roll down my window and stick my head out. "Check out my new phone. It's sick!"

Timmy skates over and looks in the window. "Sick! It is about time you got a phone. I've had mine for a year already."

"Really?"

"Yep," Timmy answers.

"What is your phone number?"

"Skater T," Bobby says looking in the window to see my new phone. "Skater D is Danny's number and Skater B is my number."

"Skater T?"

"Yes dirt wad, spell it out on the phone to get the phone number," Bobby snarls.

"Thanks for reminding me that I am a Delightfully Intelligent Respected Tween!" I say grinning.

"I called you a dirt WAD, not DIRT," Bobby teases.

"Oh, so you think I am also a Wickedly Awesome Dude!"

Everyone starts laughing, even my parents.

Danny asks Bobby, "When are you ever going to stop calling us names?"

"If this bozo doesn't stop with the comebacks I won't have a choice but to stop," Bobby grumbles under his breath.

"What's that Bobby? Did Blaze actually shut you up?" Timmy remarks playfully.

Dropping his skateboard to the ground, Bobby steps on and he begins to push off with his other foot. "Whatever. I'm outta here!"

Timmy and Danny follow Bobby, and my dad pulls into the driveway. The garage door opens slowly and he parks in the garage.

I get out and walk around to the backyard to greet Sir Licksalot. He is sitting next to the super-sized fountain in the backyard, basking in the sun with his Dingo bone lying in the grass next to him. Little splashes of water falling down from the lion's mouths splash onto him. The fountain is three tiers and made of stone. The top two tiers have stone lion faces carved into them, which is how the water flows from tier to tier. I sit on the bottom fountain rim wondering what I am going to do for the rest of the day. Then I remember that I should charge the new phone so that I can use it. I walk into the house, and as I am plugging the phone into the charger, my mom conveniently requests that I start doing my chores.

Hours later, after I have finished doing my chores, I check on my phone and see that it is fully charged and ready to be used. I send Danny a text.

"Are you still skating?"

"Who dis?

"Blaze"

"Y. U want 2 SK8?"

"Do you?"

"IDK. R U@ hm"

"Yes"

"WOW?"

"Huh?"

"world of warcraft? u shld no that."

"OH! See if the others want to play"

"they r onl"

"What?"

"They are online playing already. You need to learn text language dude."

"LOL"

"Better than B4.C U ONL"

"Bye"

I put my phone in my pocket and I hear Sir Licksalot barking in the back yard. I slowly walk back into the kitchen and look at him through the backdoor window. "What now, Sir Licksalot?" I shout.

Sir Licksalot puts his front feet on the rim of the fountain. The hair on his neck and back is standing on end, and he is barking at the water with so much force that his nose is dipping into the water with each bark. What if the fountain takes him and I never see him again? "Sir Licksalot, get down boy!" I scream frantically as I dash outside.

Sir Licksalot jumps onto the rim of the bottom tier balancing like a cat on a fence barking and growling at the water, getting louder and louder all the time.

"Sir Licksalot, get down! You are going to fall in."

Sir Licksalot slips on the wet slippery surface and he starts to fall into the water. I sprint as fast as I can to grab him before he drowns, or worse, disappears. Reaching into the water, I feel something hairy. It's the tip of his tail and I hold on to him as tightly as I can. The water starts to swirl like hot tub jets. The mouths of the lions begin to open. It is all happening just like it did the last time, when the fountain carried us far from home. As the fountain prepares to pull Sir Licksalot down to who knows where, I brace my thighs against the fountain edge, pulling on Sir Licksalot as hard as I can. Sir Licksalot flies up into the air and I fly backwards and land flat on my back. He lands on the grass on his feet, dripping from nose to tail, looking like a drowned rat. Then he shakes the water off and runs over to me. His tail is wagging fast, sending sprays of water into the air as he licks the water off my arms. My thoughts are racing as I try not to imagine what could have happened to him if I hadn't shown up when I did. Then I wonder why the fountain started to prepare for an adventure without moving the top magic ball first, as we did before. In recollection of how it happened before, I was trying to fix the fountain after my basketball knocked the top ball over. I put the fountain ball on the tube that was sticking up and I turned it to the right. Then I turned it to the left. I turned it to the right again. But it was sitting crooked. I turned it to the left and it spun around by itself very fast and before we knew it we were on our adventure into Mavericks.

Gripping Sir Licksalot's ears, I pull his face towards mine. "Boy, this is the one thing you cannot play with. The fountain will suck you in and I will never see you again. You can't find your way home without me. Don't go near the fountain!" I pat his head and then get up to go back into the house.

My mom calls out to me just as we start to enter the house. "Why are you and the dog wet?"

"Uh…umm…uh…I gave Sir Licksalot a bath and he shook the water off and got me wet too."

"Stay outside and dry him off, and yourself, before you come in," Mom demands, handing me a couple of towels.

Feeling curious I ask, "Mom were you outside earlier adding water to the fountain?"

"Yes, I was. Why?"

"Uh, the grass was all wet over there so I was just wondering."

My mind starts wandering as I dry us off. Maybe mom turned the top ball trying to clean off the bird droppings. What if my parents find out about our magic fountain? Would they destroy it if they knew what it could do?

Drying off Sir Licksalot's paws I tell him, "We have to be more careful Sir Licksalot. They might take the fountain away from us if they find out. This is way too cool, and our adventures will make for some sick summer stories. My teachers will give me good grades for using my imagination on my 'What I did over the summer' essays. As Timmy would say, 'English class is in da bag'. But for now it's our secret, so don't blow it for us."

Sir Licksalot licks the water off his paws and I rub his head. "That a boy. You are the best dog ever. I'm so glad you are a part of our family."

Something feels really weird. My pocket is moving. It's my phone vibrating. I pull it out and look at it. There is a message from Skater T.

"Where RU@, don't C U ONL"

"Drying Sir Licksalot off, he fell into the fountain."

"OMG"

"I know! Want to go to Mavericks tomorrow instead of next weekend? Trying to save Sir Licksalot made me anxious to go on an adventure now.

"Heck ya. No BFF's!"

"You mean just the guys?"

"Ya. BRB"

I wait and wait for him to respond. Then, at last (it took him long enough) he writes back.

"They R in 2"

"Who?"

"B & D. G2G, C U 2morrow

"Meet at the fountain after our parents leave for work around 9:30 in the morning."

"K"

CHAPTER 4
Magic

Waking up and wiping the sleep from my eyes as I stumble out of my room, I find the house is empty. There is a note on the table that reads:

No one is allowed in the house when we aren't home. Breakfast is in the microwave. Have a good day and we will see you tonight. Love, Mom.

The doorbell rings just as I am pulling my breakfast out of the microwave.

Sir Licksalot runs to the door barking with the fur on his neck standing on end.

I open the door and Timmy is standing there wearing a bright blue shirt, shorts, his shades, and a funny looking grin.

"Dude, why are you here so early?"

"My parents took Tabitha to her friend's house for the day and they asked if I needed a ride to my friend's house. I told them I was coming here, so they let me ride my skateboard over."

"But I can't have anyone in the house when my parents are gone. It is one of the dumbest rules ever. What if your parents tell my parents and...?"

"Don't sweat it, I told my mom and dad that we would be skating outside. I'll go play basketball in the backyard until the others get here."

Placing his ear buds in his ears, Timmy starts singing some new beat box tune and heads around to the back of the house. Just as I am closing the door, there is another knock. Opening the door, I see Danny standing there in a sunny yellow shirt and black shorts. There are all kinds of gadgets in his pockets. I swear the guy resembles a walking electronics store. I can see his GPS device, which is sticking out of his left pocket.

"Hey dude. Why is everyone so early?"

"It is 9:30 already," Danny says, giving me a look.

"Shoot. I must have over slept," I say, rubbing my eyes. Danny begins to walk into the house. "I'm sorry Danny, I'm not allowed to let anyone in the house when my parents aren't here. Can you hang out with Timmy in the backyard? I will be out as soon as I get dressed."

"So much for eating my breakfast. At least you got to eat yours," I mumble to Sir Licksalot as I walk through the kitchen. Sir Licksalot licks his lips with his long skinny tongue and he gives a loud belch. "That's my boy!"

As I walk into my bedroom trying to decide what clothes I should wear, I hear the back gate slam closed. That must be Bobby. Soon I hear the sound of people arguing coming from the backyard. I quickly put on a pair of blue jean shorts, a pair of shoes, and I grab a red tank top from my drawer.

Trying to get my shirt on over my head, I realize my hair isn't even brushed, but I can't ignore all the noise in the backyard any longer. Sprinting to the backdoor, I open it and ask, "What's going on? What's the problem out here?"

"Bobby brought Cici," Timmy replies with a tone of anger in his voice.

"I don't get what the big deal is," Cici says.

"The big deal is that we said no girls this time. When we had to go looking for you girls the last time, we almost died," Danny says. "I didn't bring Jesse, and Timmy didn't bring Tabitha. It's supposed to be just the guys."

"Why did you bring Cici, Bobby?" I ask.

"It isn't any of your business," Bobby says grumpily.

"Uh yeah, I think it is our business. We want to have fun, not baby sit," Timmy grumbles.

"If I didn't bring her Cici was going to tell my parents about our secret. That is why she is here," Bobby explains.

With her hand on her hip Cici chimes in. "I thought we were the Fools. All of us, not just you boys."

Trying to answer her in a way that won't upset her I say, "We are, but this time we agreed that it would be just the guys. You know, guy bonding time."

"If you guys don't want my sister here, then you don't want me here either," Bobby says, turning to leave. I have no idea why he is being so difficult.

"Really, Bobby? We don't want to argue with you today. If you go, you go. If you don't, you don't," Timmy says.

Looking over at the guys, as they stand there looking angry with their arms crossed, I decide to play peacemaker. "Cici can go with us. One girl has to be easier to keep track of than all of them."

"Fine. Just make sure she stays with us this time," Danny says.

Batting her blue eyes at Timmy, Cici adds, "I will. I promise to stay right next to Bobby the whole time. I won't be any trouble at all. I swear!"

Timmy mumbles, "Uh hmm."

Cici walks over to the fountain asking, "Is everyone ready to go?"

"No. I just woke up like fifteen minutes ago. All the arguing brought me out here before I could do my hair, brush my teeth, or even eat my breakfast."

"I thought something smelled disgusting out here," Bobby says chuckling.

"Funny. Give me five minutes," I call out as I hurry back into the house.

Back in the house, I try to get my hair to cooperate as I take random bites of my breakfast burrito. Looking into the mirror I mouth with my lips, "Bring it on." Turning the bathroom light off, I head towards the back door.

Closing the back door, I walk over quickly to the fountain.

Everyone is sitting on the edge of the fountain. Cici is swirling a purple flower back and forth in the water.

"Where do you want to go first, Riptide or Wipeout?" I ask.

"I bet we will land in the rip tide" Timmy says.

"I don't know. Let's ask the crystal ball," Bobby says sarcastically as he moves the top ball of the fountain to the right, then to the left. Bobby says, "Take me to..."

Still swirling the delicate flower in the water, Cici completes Bobby's thought: "...somewhere tropical for my tenth birthday."

Bobby is still turning the ball of the fountain back to the right and one last time to the left. Then its spins around really fast and the water begins to swirl around like a water tornado. We hear, "Oha."

Sir Licksalot hears the raging water and he races to the fountain, barking as loudly as he can. In the next moment we are sucked into the fountain and the velocity is pulling us into the swirling water. Sir Licksalot jumps in to save me, grabbing hold of my shorts with his teeth. We are all spinning around in the water, getting sucked down into the stem of the spiral. Soon we are all lying on our backs, each of us a human luge, sliding along a slippery tube of water that seems to be miles and miles long, moving at speeds of one hundred and fifty miles per hour. I do all I can to rise up to a sitting position so that I can grab Sir Licksalot, who is still biting the leg of my shorts. Trying to calm him, I pry his mouth open to get him to let go of my shorts, and then I place him in my arms like a football and hold on tight. Sir Licksalot's long floppy ears cover his eyes.

Timmy yells out, "This rocks!"

Bobby, who is right behind me, looks as if he is going to pass out. I can see the white knuckles of his clenched fists crossed against his chest. Danny raises his right arm and gives me a thumbs up. I can hear the faint echoes of Cici's voice because she is screaming at the top of her lungs, but I cannot see her in the darkness ahead. Suddenly, we are moving upwards, a blast of very hot air pushing us out into the open air. We land heavily, rolling around in black and red dust. When I finally come to a stop, I sit up and look around. Sir Licksalot shakes off all the dirt, creating a miniature dust cloud.

As the dust clears I ask, "Where on earth are we? It is absolutely freezing here!"

Bobby sits up and starts laughing hysterically.

"What's so funny?" I ask.

"Your new hairstyle," Bobby jokes.

Timmy and Danny sit up and they start cracking up too.

"What? It can't be that bad, it's just dirt. You guys are dirty too."

"You just had to put your gel in," Bobby giggles.

"The humidity, the blasting air, and the gel are making your hair stand on end, literally. Every single strand," Danny says, holding up a lens from Timmy's broken sun glasses so that I can see what I look like.

Laughing uncontrollably, Bobby blurts out, "You look like you put your finger in a light socket."

Looking down at my clothes I ask, "What is this stuff?

"It looks like black soot from a fireplace," Danny remarks.

"Do any of you see Cici?" Bobby suddenly asks.

We all get up to look for her and Sir Licksalot starts sniffing around the area.

"I knew we shouldn't have come. Something bad always happens!" Bobby says. A panicky tone is creeping into his voice.

"I'm sure she is around somewhere. I heard her screaming on the way here," Timmy says, trying to be reassuring.

"Did you hear yourself? You said screaming. That means something happened to her," Bobby says, biting his fingernails and looking around.

Grabbing Bobby's shirt I shake him and tell him, "Dude, snap out of it. We will find her. I thought you were a tough guy?"

"I am the smart guy! I knew that coming here was a bad idea. You always have such stupid ideas and you look like a spooky alien," Bobby snarls.

"Dude, why are you being so mean? They are just trying to help you calm down," Danny interrupts.

Bobby shouts out, "I don't need help, and I don't need a De Ta De blabbing in my face."

With a smile on my face, I jump at the opportunity to put Bobby in his place. "I always knew Danny was a Diagnosed Expert Tweeter and Digital Extraordinaire."

"What a great compliment, Bobby. I didn't know you had it in you," Danny says happily.

Pointing at me with a very dirty finger, Bobby says, "You are the most annoying person I ever met. Your only purpose in life is to be annoying!"

I can't resist saying, "Don't trip chocolate chip."

Everyone is laughing and Bobby's eyebrows are down, his lips are pursed, and he looks as if he is about to explode.

"Relax already! Cici has to be around here somewhere. By the way, has anyone seen Sir Licksalot?"

Just then I hear the faint sound of echoing barks. We look at each other and begin to run towards the sound.

CHAPTER 5
10,000 Feet

Taking in our surroundings as we run towards the barking, all we see are mini hills that look like gigantic ant hills. The ground appears to be covered with ash, dust, rock and red dirt.

Danny stops us. "Wait a minute. Look around. Do you know where we are?"

"Uh . . . no! Obviously we aren't at Mavericks," Bobby remarks sarcastically.

"We are in the crater of a volcano. Those mini hills are cinder cones," Danny says. Dusting back ash from his hands he says, "This is volcanic ash, and the red dirt is from the lava."

Pulling out one of his gadgets, Danny continues. "Check it out. My waterproof 76CSX GPS barometric altimeter indicates that we are 10,000 feet above sea level."

Timmy shivers and he rubs his arms. "Explains why it is so freakin' cold."

"If that thing can't tell us where Cici is, then what good is it?" Bobby grumbles in frustration.

"It can do all kinds of amazing things. It can tell us exactly how to get to where we want to go," Danny interjects.

"Okay wise one. We don't even know where we are, let alone where we want to go, so how is it going to tell us how to get there?" Bobby asks.

"He has a legitimate point, Danny," I say.

"I downloaded a lot of maps but still had more to download. I thought I had more time before we would go again. Maybe the map for this location wasn't downloaded yet. Hmm. The GPS doesn't seem to have a reading for where we are." In a concerned voice, Danny tells us, "It sort of looks like we are on an island."

"How do you know that?" I ask.

Looking up at us Danny says, "Because there is a large body of water all around us," as he turns the GPS towards us so that we can look at it.

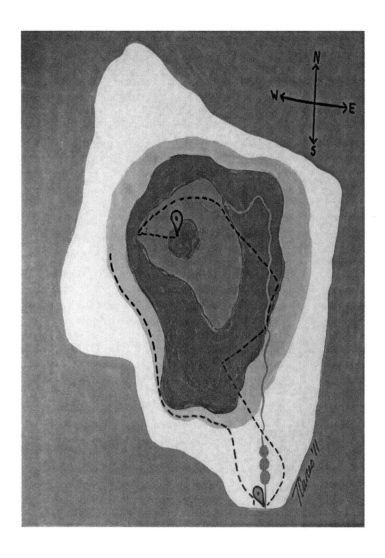

Looking at the map, Bobby starts to hyperventilate.

"Dude, what's wrong?" Timmy asks Bobby.

Bobby doesn't say anything as he continues to breathe heavily from his fear of heights and sharks in the ocean.

Folding his left hand into a fist and placing it over his mouth, Timmy starts to beat box. He points at Bobby with his right hand and sings:

> **Chicka Bhoo,**
> **He's**
> **Chicka Bhoo, Bhoo**
> **a**
> **Chicka Bhoo, Bhoo**
> **Chicken!**

Moving his arms in the motion of the chicken dance, Timmy continues,

> **Bawk baa baa bawk!**

Catching his breath for a brief moment, Bobby yells out, "Quiet Pork Chop!"

"What's the matter Bobby? Are you jealous because he is the Predefined Original Rappin' Kid," I ask.

Timmy interrupts me before I can continue. "Or is it because I am a Charismatic Hunk of Popularity!"

Bobby shakes his head in disgust. "Unbelievable! Now you have Timmy talking like you, Blaze."

Sir Licksalot's barking starts getting louder and closer. I shout out to him, "Sir Licksalot, over here boy!"

Coming around from behind one of the cinder cones is Sir Licksalot, and Cici is right behind him.

Bobby shouts out in excitement. "It's Cici!"

Sir Licksalot runs up, sniffs us, and then he goes in the other direction with his tail between his legs. I think this is the first time, ever, that he hasn't licked someone or something.

Looking at Cici, I ask, "Where were you?"

Cici shrugs her shoulders up to her ears and she puts her hands up in the air. "I don't know. Sir Licksalot found me, so I just followed him. I figured you guys were close by."

I turn to look at Sir Licksalot and notice that he is running back and forth, sniffing every square inch of the ground. I think that he is looking for a Dingo bone. Sir Licksalot comes upon some bushes that have spear-shaped leaves covered in little silver hairs. The bushes are about two feet wide and some are taller than me. Some have dozens and dozens of tiny flowers on a stalk so they kind of look like a giant purple corn on the cob. Sir Licksalot smells all around one of the plants and then he sticks his nose under the bottom leaves. He begins to dig with his front paws.

Cici starts laughing, pointing at me. "What happened to you?" Then looking at Bobby, still giggling, she tells him, "You look like you rolled around in the barbeque."

Cici herself is completely covered in red dirt.

"I wouldn't talk, you look like a hot tamale," Bobby shares.

Putting one hand on her hip and the other hand on the back of her head Cici remarks, "You wish you were hot like me?"

Timmy tries to get some words out, but he can't stop laughing.

Cici asks, "What's so funny Timmy?"

Timmy just shakes his head and says, "Nothing, you are 'hot' all right."

Danny and I begin laughing too as we clue into Timmy's sarcasm.

Sir Licksalot comes over and lies down next to my feet with his paws completely covered in soot. He starts whimpering.

"Shhsh. Quiet Sir Licksalot."

Bobby speaks up, "We need to decide which way to go."

Danny hits a button on his GPS. "From the map it looks like we are on the north side of the volcano right now. Maybe we should head towards the east to try to find some water and get cleaned up. It looks like there is a river in that direction. If we want to get warmer we should head downhill."

Sir Licksalot whimpers louder. We look down at him and I see that he has something in his mouth. His tail is wagging really fast, making a dust cloud.

"What do you have boy?" I ask, reaching down to retrieve it from his mouth.

Cici gives her opinion. "It looks like a pocket book."

"Nah, really?" Bobby comments.

"Clean it off and let's see what it is," Cici says.

I dust off the cover of the book. "It's illegible. It's so badly scratched up by someone's paws," I say looking down at Sir Licksalot.

"Give it to me," Bobby demands.

We all look over Bobby's shoulders and read the first page simultaneously. "The Myths."

"This is so cool. I will have something entertaining to read while you guys figure out how to get us down from this mountain," Cici joyfully snickers.

Shivering, Danny asks, "Can we start heading down and east to find some water to get cleaned up and get a little warmer?"

I nod at Danny in agreement.

Bobby turns and starts to walk in the direction that Cici came from. Danny hollers out, "You are going the wrong way."

"How do you know? Your lame GPS can't even tell us where we are," Bobby groans.

"Using the custom point of interest function, I can certainly get it to show us how to get down from this volcano. I will put it in simulator mode like this and then press the menu button. Then I scroll down to sea level. After I press enter, my GPS will create a route from here to the bottom of the mountain. Check it out, there are two paths that we can follow," Danny says as he turns to go in the direction of the river. "Come on. Let's try this route."

Eager to get cleaned off, I am right behind him with Sir Licksalot walking by my side.

Bobby and Cici look at each other, shrug their shoulders in utter confusion, and eventually they follow us. Timmy is still standing around, trying to put his sun glasses back together. "Hey, wait up!"

CHAPTER 6
The Myths

What feels like hours later Danny looks at his GPS. "It looks as if there are still miles to go," he says. "Just a short walk," he adds with a sarcastic tone and smile.

Everyone groans.

"We've already walked for hours," Timmy complains.

"No we haven't. Quit being a cry baby," Bobby replies.

I turn to Bobby and just as I am starting to say something Bobby speaks. "Don't even think about a comeback or I will squash you right here,"

Bobby warns.

"Look! Straight ahead. Check it out. Those are some weird looking trees," Cici points out.

"If there are living trees, then there is water near," I say with a giant smile on my face.

Bobby starts laughing.

"What's so funny now?" I ask.

"You," Bobby mumbles.

"Your face is so dirty and your hair is so wild you look like a cave man with glowing white teeth," Timmy explains.

"Actually what Timmy is trying to say is that you look like Wyle Coyote after an explosion that has gone wrong," Bobby clarifies.

As we tread our way through a wilderness of humungous Banyan trees with gigantic roots growing out of the ground, everyone is laughing. Except me.

As it starts to get slightly warmer, Timmy begins to huff and puff, and his face gets covered with sweat. "Can we stop for a minute to rest?" Timmy asks.

"Only for a minute," Bobby says.

Cici reaches over to Bobby and asks, "Can I have the book? I want to read it while we wait for Timmy to catch his breath."

Danny adds, "I want to hear the story too. It's a very small book. We can just sit here for a little bit and Cici can read the story to us."

I don't hesitate to give my input. "That's a good idea. The book may have some clues as to where in the world we are."

Handing the book to Cici, Bobby says, "Whatever. This book is like a million years old. Someone must have dropped it here."

"Who would hang out in a volcano crater? Timmy asks.

Cici sits down and reminds us, "Sir Licksalot did dig it up. Maybe it really is a million years old."

Bobby looks down at Cici, "Oh. Okay genius." Bobby then mimics Cici's way of speaking and he says, "If it is a million years old it would not have English written in it."

"Whatever. You were the first person to talk about it being very old," Cici reminds Bobby.

"Can we stop with all the fighting and cheap shots? Let's sit a spell and find out what is in the book," I say.

"Sit a spell? Dude, where are you from?" Timmy asks.

Bobby answers Timmy. "Retardville."

Everyone, but me of course, is laughing hysterically.

Cici still giggling asks, "Are you guys done now? Can I read?"

Timmy sits down behind Cici, using her back as a backrest. Bobby and Danny sit down the same way, with their backs to each other. Sir Licksalot jumps into Cici's lap. I'm standing up with my arms crossed. I am still upset with Bobby. I don't understand why he has to be so insulting all the time.

"Timmy looks up at me. "Dude, chilax."

"To get respect, you have to give respect," I angrily mention, looking right at Bobby.

Bobby rolls his eyes. I give him a dirty look and remain standing with my arms crossed.

Cici starts to read the book:

Let me begin by saying that there are many myths about the three Goddesses that I am about to introduce you to. Because they are such powerful Goddesses, many forms of each Goddess exist throughout the islands. You are about to read my interpretation of the stories about these divine spirits. The stories as told by my ancestors have been passed down from person to person through the years.

Pele is the Goddess of Fire and Volcanoes. In ancient chants, Goddess Pele is described as being 'She who shapes the sacred land.' Pele has long thick dark hair that has a red fiery glow. The upper part of her body is that of a young strong woman. The base of her body is the peak of a volcano and it is illuminated by the fire below.

When Pele arrived on land, she would open a crater with her magic stick, which is called a Pa-oa. Volcanoes would erupt, sending dark clouds into the sky. Pele was always chased away from the land by the Goddess of Water and the Sea, who would flood her pits snuffing out her flame. However, Pele continued to light fires, trying to make a home for herself. Pele eventually landed on Haleakala where a substantial lava flow blew out from her fire pit. Her sister the Goddess of Water and the Sea saw the huge cloud in the sky, and soon the goddesses fought one another in a battle. Pele lost and was chased away. She now rests on the southern slopes of the big island where the Goddess of water cannot reach her.

Pele, considered destructive and violent because of her fire and energy, requested forgiveness for killing mortals. Pele filled the empty branches of shrub trees that lined the lava beds with spectacular fragile red Ohi'a flowers. Pele teaches us that we have the inner power to shape our own lives with positive thoughts and actions.

Laka is the Goddess of the Hula. She happens to be Pele's favorite younger sister. Laka has beautiful long black hair and long slender arms. The upper part of her body is made up of blooming flowers. Her legs are a waterfall flowing gracefully between vines and shrubs.

One day Pele asked Laka to entertain her because she was bored. Laka wanted to please her sister so she told her a story, using body language, that described an event that they had experienced together. Using her hands, she demonstrated the motion of the wind and the waterfalls. With her fingers, she outlined the trees and flowers. She used her hips to sway to the sound of the ocean waves. Pele was pleased with her sister's entertaining talent and that day the hula was born.

Laka combines all the gifts of nature and shares them through dance. Goddess Laka's purpose is to honor nature and unite all living entities that live on the land. Laka teaches us that honoring those we cherish with unselfish love will bring much happiness into our lives. She also wants us to learn that our talents are a gift. If we want to develop our talents we must believe in ourselves, use our imagination, and take chances without fear.

Goddess of the Moon

Hina lived beneath the shadow of the crater, in a cave that was located behind a very large waterfall where the rushing river fell into a sacred pool. In this place, Hina pounded her kapa and prepared food, while caring for her family.

Hina worked very long days without help. Her husband was lazy, and her children took her work for granted. She eventually became tired of her life. One day Hina saw a beautiful rainbow rise from the sacred pool, up through the clouds and into the heavens. She looked up to the heavens, wishing she could escape from her life on the land. She began to climb the rainbow through the slippery mist of the clouds. The sun began to beat down on her back. She continued to crawl, but the heat of the sun weakened her strength and Hina slid down the rainbow back to the Earth. After the sun set, Hina began to regain her strength. As the light from the full moon shone down upon her, the rainbow suddenly reappeared. When the full moon completely rose, she declared, "I will climb to the moon and find rest." Hina took her calabash and started to climb up the rainbow. Her husband caught a glimpse of her and shouted out to her, "Do not go into the heavens." She responded by saying, "My mind is made up." Hina continued to climb, higher and higher, until she was almost out of reach. Hina's husband jumped into the air, catching her leg. She tried to shake him off, but he was too strong for her. Afraid that he would prevent her escape, Hina used all her strength to continue to climb and her leg broke off in her husband's hand. Hina reached the stars chanting very loudly, and after a long journey, she eventually arrived at the Moon where she rested with her calabash next to her.

Hina is the Goddess of the moon. She is a breathtaking silhouette of a mother who sits in the center of the moon. With her hair lying gently on her shoulders, her thick eyebrows and full lips define her face as she looks down upon the Earth. The base of her body is her kapa, the silver lining in the clouds. Her purpose is to watch over the world from high above, providing healing and protection for those who are mistreated.

Hina teaches us that with hard work and ambition, there is a pot of gold waiting for everyone at the end of the rainbow. She reminds us that no one, and nothing, can hold us back from obtaining our goals, unless we allow it.

As unique as the Goddesses are, each one serves a significant purpose on Earth. Pele shapes it, Hina protects it, Laka honors it. We, the mortals, continue to live off it. In essence, we are all connected with the development of the planet we call Earth.

"Ok that's deep," Bobby says.

"I think it's dope," Timmy says, flicking his hand out.

"You would since you are a dope!" Bobby remarks.

The ground trembles and we all look at each other as the echo of a rumble gets louder and closer. In the distance, we see that a herd of wild pigs are running straight towards us. It's a pig stampede!

CHAPTER 7
Terror

"Climb the banyan tree!" I scream.

As I am scrambling as fast as I can to climb the tree, I call out to Sir Licksalot. "Run boy!" Sir Licksalot sprints towards me, but then he looks back. Sir Licksalot, being the tough dog he is, turns and stands his ground to protect the book that Cici dropped on the ground. He barks ferociously at the pigs. The pigs circle him and he is trapped! Sir Licksalot is surrounded and I begin to panic. "Come on guys we have to help him. The pigs will kill him if we don't do something fast."

"What do you have in mind?" Danny asks, looking down at Sir Licksalot from the tree.

"I don't know. We have to distract the pigs. We need to get their attention away from Sir Licksalot."

"How exactly are we going to do that without getting ourselves killed? Bobby asks as he sits perched in the tree.

"I have an idea. What if we all jump out of the tree and run in different directions?" Timmy asks.

"Not only are you a dope, you are nuts too!" Bobby says.

"No. He is right," Cici says. "Sir Licksalot is being very brave. We cannot abandon him."

"If we jump down and run in different directions then the pigs will chase us and forget about Sir Licksalot. We are a bigger moving target to them. Sir Licksalot would just be a snack."

Cici's face gets a pale look, "Gross Blaze."

Danny says, "I'm in."

"Me too," Cici nervously discloses.

"I'm in. I think," Timmy mumbles as he looks down at the pig's tusks.

"Not me. I am not risking my life for a dumb dog," Bobby says.

"All you think about is yourself Bobby. You don't consider anyone else. You have to be the most selfish person I have ever met." I am so mad at Bobby I can hardly stand it.

"Well, if you are going to be like that, why should I help you?" Bobby asks.

"Whoever is going to help, we have about two seconds left before those pigs charge at Sir Licksalot. We go on three," I say, glaring at Bobby.

Just then a pig charges at Sir Licksalot. Sir Licksalot doesn't cower down, even though the pig is coming straight towards him, snorting with his head down. Then the pig slips on the book and he slides into Sir Licksalot. Sir Licksalot yelps as the tip of the tusk pokes him in the rear end.

"THREE!" Cici yells out.

We all jump down out of the tree – except for Bobby – and run in different directions, dodging the tree roots as fast as we can. Most of the pigs chase us, opening the circle of terror just enough so that Sir Licksalot can escape. In a flash, Sir Licksalot snatches the book and runs as fast as he can away from the pigs.

A couple of stubborn pigs sniffed out Bobby, circling the base of the tree, snorting, and scuffing the ground with their hooves. "Help me!" Bobby starts squealing.

I have half a mind to leave him. Looking around for the others, I holler back, "Karma, my friend, karma!"

"You can't leave me here," Bobby cries out, trembling so much that the tree branch he is sitting on is shaking too.

"Oh yes I can. You would leave me in a second. You only want to be our friend when it is convenient for you," I say.

"I'm selfish. I admit it," Bobby yells back. "I don't know why I am."

"It's because you want all the attention. Well now you have it," Danny shouts out.

In a shaky voice, Bobby tries again. "Help me, please!"

"Only if you lighten up and change your attitude. You didn't have to come today, you chose to come," Timmy shouts out.

"You can choose to be mean to us or you can pull the stick out of your rump and be a real friend," I add.

"Yeah you need a royal attitude adjustment or an anger management class," Danny says.

"I get it! I get it! I am sorry! Now get me out of here," Bobby begs.

I chuckle and say, "Just stop moving and they will forget about you and leave."

"Are you kidding me?" Bobby mumbles.

Timmy answers. "Nope, now who's the dope?"

"You made your point, now quiet down so they leave," Bobby says, still shaking and with his legs and arms wrapped around the tree branch.

Fifteen to twenty minutes pass by. I quietly move over to Timmy, who is hiding behind the trunk of a huge Banyan tree. Danny eventually joins us. The remaining pigs start to get discouraged and wander off. Bobby slowly climbs down out of the tree. We walk over towards him, which is when he starts looking around. He runs over to some of the trees and looks behind them. He has this weird look on his face.

"What now?" Danny asks.

"Dude, what is your problem?" Timmy asks.

Bobby gives a big swallow. "Where is Cici?"

Feeling alarmed, we all start looking around, which is when I realize that Sir Licksalot is missing too. "Did anyone see where Sir Licksalot ran off too?

"That's a negative," Timmy replies.

"He's probably with Cici again," Danny answers.

"Please be together," Bobby says quietly to himself, with a little optimism in his voice.

Looking at his GPS and then at the terrain, Danny makes a suggestion. "We can either follow the map into the wilderness or continue to head to the river. Cici knew we were heading to the river so she should go that way too."

"There is no way I am hanging out in this wilderness," Bobby says.

"The river it is," Danny says turning towards the east. "Follow me."

Not having any better ideas we shrug our shoulders and follow.

"Maybe we should make a plan," Bobby mentions.

"Like what?" Danny asks.

"If we don't find Cici and Sir Licksalot in the next hour then we split up and two of us trek back and take the other path through the wilderness," Bobby explains.

"Fine. But I am Blaze's partner. I can't believe you brought her again and we have to find her rather than have a good time now!" Timmy remarks very annoyed.

"Whatever, it doesn't matter. All that matters is that we find them soon. What if one of the pigs hurt Cici with its tusk and she is bleeding, or worse, dying?" Bobby asks in tremendous despair.

I didn't consider the serious danger of nature. Now I am really afraid for both Sir Licksalot and Cici. "Let's not waste any time!" I say not wanting to show any fear, even though I am full of panic now that Bobby put that scary thought in my head. Who knows what else is out here that can hurt us.

CHAPTER 8
Wilderness

After running and running for what feels like miles, Cici finally slows down. She looks around, but the boys and Sir Licksalot are nowhere in sight. "Hello? Is anyone out there?" Cici calls out. Soon she finds a path that winds around the trees and down the hillside, which she decides to follow. Feeling frustrated, she repeatedly calls out, "Hello?" as she walks down the path.

Her voice carries with an echo, but there is no response. After a while, she calls out once again. "Is anyone out here?" She continues walking until she comes to a place where there are all kinds of beautiful flowering plants, and trees with blossoms on them. As she gets closer, she notices a movement near one of the trees.

"Hello?" She calls out in a shaky voice.

This time she gets a response. "Aloha." A pretty girl with dark hair and shining eyes steps out from behind a tree. She has a lei of yellow flowers around her neck.

Relieved that she is dealing with a person and not a pig, Cici reaches her hand out to introduce herself. "I am Cici. What's your name?"

Removing the lei from her neck, the young girl places the lei around Cici's neck. "My name is Alana."

Cici smells the flowers around her neck. "Thank you. The flowers smell so good and they are so pretty, just like you."

"Mahalo," Alana says with a smile.

"I'm sorry I don't know what that means," Cici says, feeling a little embarrassed.

"Maholo means thank you in my language," Alana explains.

Alana is the same height as Cici and they look approximately the same age. Cici stares at Alana as she watches the girl delicately pick flowers. She watches Alana's long dark brown hair dance in the mild breeze. Alana's flawless skin is a shimmering bronze color. She is wearing a blue wrap around skirt with white flowers printed on it, and a matching bikini top. Her feet are bare, and she is carrying a large basket that is full of leaves and flowers.

"Why are you picking the flowers?" Cici asks.

"For the luau," Alana answers.

"What is a luau?"

"A giant feast. We will eat Pua'a," Alana says.

"Pua'a?"

"Pig. They are roasting the Pua'a in the imu right now near the sacred pools," Alana explains.

"What is an imu?" Cici asks.

"An underground oven. The men in my family dig a pit in the sand in the morning. Wood and round river rocks are put into the pit. The wood is lit on fire and after a while, the river rock becomes very hot. Then we place sweet banana stalks over the rock with banana leaves on top. This makes a bed for the pig to lie on to cook. We cover the pig with more banana leaves and Ti leaves. Then the pit is covered with a tarp and we put sand on top of that to seal the heat in."

"Wild pigs tried to attack us!" Cici tells Alana.

"Us?" Alana inquires.

"My brother and his friends and a little dog named Sir Licksalot are here with me," Cici explains.

"Where are they?" Alana asks, looking around.

"When the pigs attacked us we all ran in different directions. I think I'm lost," Cici explains.

"Help me to finish picking the pua for the luau and then I will take you to the sacred pools. Everyone will meet by the sacred pools tonight. I have a feeling that your brother and friends will find their way to the pools soon," Alana tells Cici.

"How can you be sure of that?" Cici asks. "They don't know their way around."

"It is just a feeling I have," Alana says, smiling at Cici. "If they don't find their way to the pools, my family will look for them."

"Cool. Thank you," Cici says feeling very relieved.

Then Alana shows Cici how to gently pick the flowers so that they are not damaged.

"How come all your words sound alike?" Cici asks, recalling what Alana called the flowers in her language.

"We only have sixteen letters in our alphabet. When using the English alphabet we only have twelve letters," Alana explains. "When we speak, A is pronounced 'ah', E is pronounced 'eh', I is pronounced 'ee', O is pronounced 'oh', U is pronounced 'oo'."

"Oh." Cici pauses, thinking. "How do you know such good English?"

"A lovely lady visited the islands many years ago. When she couldn't understand what we were saying, she decided to stay here and teach us English. My ancestors learned from her, and now all the children on the islands know English well. I like to practice writing English in a book that I have, but I lost it a while ago," Alana tells Cici, with a sad look crossing her face.

Cici asks, "Where are we?"

"You are on Haleakala which means, House by the sun. Haleakala is almost the largest volcano in the world, and it is on eastern Maui, which is one of the Hawaiian islands. The world's largest volcano is Mauna Loa on the Big Island, and it is still active today. That is where Goddess Pele lives now," Alana explains with a smile.

Cici gets a great big smile on her face and starts dancing around screaming out, "I'm in Hawaii! I can't believe it. I am in Hawaii! This is the best birthday present ever."

"Hau`oli lā hānau," Alana says looking at Cici.

Cici shrugs her shoulders, not understanding Alana's words. "Huh?"

"Happy Birthday," Alana says, smiling at Cici. Then she takes Cici's hand and guides her down the path. "I'll take you to the sacred pools."

Being curious, Cici asks, "What are the sacred pools?"

"There are twenty-four waterfalls that spill into pools of different heights and depths. One of the sacred pools is located right in front of Goddess Hina's cave. That is the general area where we are going to have our luau tonight."

"This is so awesome. Can I swim there?"

"Yes, but only to purify. If you disturb anything, you will witness Goddess Hina's wrath," Alana warns.

Cici doesn't dare ask what Alana means. She isn't about to spoil her dream day by thinking about unpleasant things. The girls continue along the path.

"We found a book in the crater that mentions the Goddess Hina in it. I only got to read the first few pages before the pigs came," Cici tells Alana as they walk down the trail.

"A book?" Alana asks eagerly.

"Yes a book about Goddesses. Kinda like a pocket book, just a little bigger than our hands," Cici explains.

"The one who has the divine book will be protected by the Goddesses."

"Really?" Cici asks looking at Alana oddly.

"The essence of the Goddesses is within the book," Alana says.

"You mean the book we found is yours?" Cici asks.

"Yes. I am sure of it."

CHAPTER 9
The Encounter

On the other side of the mountain, Danny, Timmy, Bobby and I stumble across Sir Licksalot's paw prints as we travel down the mountainside.

Danny points to the ground. "Dude, check it out. Those prints are fresh and really small."

"Sir Licksalot has to be ahead of us," I say optimistically.

"Cici better be with him or I will..." Bobby adds.

"You will what Bobby? Blame us as usual?" I interrupt.

"Chill out Blaze. I was going to say, I will be very worried. This mountain is humungous and there are a gazillion places where she could be. She could be anywhere."

"Cici is a smart girl. If she isn't with Sir Licksalot she will find her way to the river," Danny says.

"Quiet," Timmy interrupts.

"Why?" I ask.

"Do you hear that?" Timmy asks.

Faintly we hear birds chirping. We pick up our pace and jog forward. Soon we see Sir Licksalot. He is in a grove of trees that are covered with bright flowers, and he is busily trotting around, following some honeycreeper birds. They are so tiny and so colorful. One kind of bird has bright red plumes, a short and slightly curved black bill, and white feathers underneath its tail. A group of these birds are flying in and out of the trees drinking nectar from the red blossoms. Another kind of bright red bird has a long curved orange bill so that it can get the nectar from the tubular flowers. There are some honeycreepers with speckled green dark feathers too. As we walk further into the grove of flowering trees, a flock of bright yellow birds gather together, teasing Sir Licksalot, who is watching them.

"These birds are amazing," Danny says. "That is the Parrotbill. See the one with a parrot-like beak? It has a light stripe above the eye," he adds, pointing to a bird.

"That one right there?" Timmy asks, pointing to the same bird.

"Yes," Danny responds. "It is endangered. There are only about five hundred left."

"How do you know so much smarty pants?" Bobby asks.

"I pay attention in class. We just learned about endangered species, duh!" Danny teases Bobby.

"Their beak is big and strong, which allows them to pry open twigs and other plants to get insects and grubs," Danny tells us.

"Grub?! I am up for some grub!" Timmy chimes in, rubbing his belly.

We all laugh really loud, scaring the birds away.

"Cici are you here? Cici!" Bobby calls out.

No answer. Bobby is visibly frustrated and scared.

Sir Licksalot comes trotting over. I bend down to pat his head. I notice that he has something in his mouth. "I can't believe it. Sir Licksalot still has the book of the myths."

"I bet he wishes it was a Dingo bone, like I wish there were fruits on these trees instead of these dumb flowers," Timmy says, as he picks one of the flowers.

At that very moment the trees start to sway and the wind picks up. Without any warning, hard rain starts to fall. I feel as if the forest wants to swallow us up. The rain is blowing sideways as if it wants to wash us away. We all run as fast as we can to get back on the path. Sir Licksalot is sprinting right beside us.

"Remember the story Cici started reading us about Goddess Pele's sacred flowers. Guess what? That was a lava bed, and those must have been her flowers!" I tell Timmy.

"Who cares? Let's get out of here!" Bobby screams out, picking up his pace.

We run at least a mile or so until we find ourselves in a place where there is lush tall green grass, ferns, and thick ground cover. A warm misty drizzle falls from the sky through the branches of dozens of strange looking trees. Each tree has above ground roots that keep it propped up. The roots look like thin tree trunks, with at least fifty of them per tree reaching down to the ground and creating a web of roots that looks almost like a cage. The leaves are long, with fruit hanging in the middle of them. The fruits look like enormous upside down pineapple tops.

"Stop. I can't go any further," Timmy calls out as he tries to catch his breath. Then he collapses and lies flat on his back in the grass. "My heart hurts. I am going to die," Timmy adds.

"You are not going to die. You are just out of shape," Bobby says.

Sir Licksalot lies next to Timmy, panting really hard.

Danny pulls out his GPS. "Guys we are only a few hundred feet away from the river. Come on, let's just go a little further so that we can get cleaned up and get a drink of water.

"Sure," I say.

Bobby, desperate to find Cici, nods in agreement thinking she may be at the river already waiting for them.

Timmy, on the other hand, does not move. "Ah, come on. I'm tired, and I need food."

Just them Timmy opens his eyes and he sees the fruit on the trees.

"Is this a mirage or is that fruit I see?" Timmy asks rising up on his elbows.

"I'd say that is fruit dude," I answer with a smile.

"Help me up the tree," Timmy tells Bobby.

"Why me?" Bobby asks.

"You are always showing off your muscles, so boost me up," Timmy demands.

Bobby laces his fingers and creates a cup with his hands so that Timmy has a place to put his foot.

"On the count of three. One..." Timmy shouts out.

Bobby doesn't wait. Instead, he hoists Timmy into the air. Timmy reaches up to grab the leaves for balance as he reaches for the fruit, "Ouch! Ouch! Put me down, put me down!"

"What's the problem now?" Bobby asks.

Timmy shows him his hand. He has scratches from the spikes on the leaves.

"Well that will teach you to stop thinking about your stomach all the time," Bobby jokes.

"Blaze, will you stand next to Bobby so that you can both boost me up giving me more balance so I don't have to hold onto the leaves?" Timmy asks.

"Sure," I say walking over to them.

Bobby and I both lace our fingers together and cup our hands. Timmy steps into our hands and he uses our shoulders to keep himself balanced. We quickly lift him as high as possible and Danny shouts out directions, "Move a little to the right. Now back some. No move forward a little. Now to the left."

Timmy is reaching for the fruit and Bobby and I keep following Danny's directions.

"I got one! Put me down," Timmy finally shouts out.

We lower Timmy down. The fruit is a green oblong thing that is about six inches wide and ten inches long. It is covered with wedges.

"Do you think I can eat it?" Timmy asks.

"I don't know. It doesn't look ripe," Danny responds.

"I didn't do all that work for nothing. You better eat it," Bobby says.

I pull on one of the wedges and out pops a key sized piece of fruit. The outside ring in the flesh is green, then the next ring is a red orange color, and in middle the fruit is a canary yellow.

"Try it" I say, handing the piece over to Timmy.

Timmy cautiously takes a bite. I fully expect to see Timmy spit the fruit out, but instead he doesn't react at all.

"Dude, are you ok?" I ask.

"Mmm hmmm," Timmy responds.

"Well, what does it taste like?" Bobby asks.

"Coconut and almonds. All I need is chocolate and I'd have an Almond Joy!" Timmy says with a dreamy look on his face.

"Are you going to share it with us, or eat it all by yourself?" Bobby inquires.

"Try it, you guys will like it," Timmy says, holding the fruit up so that everyone can get their own wedge.

When Sir Licksalot is fully rested, he gets up and starts wandering around smelling everything. While we are eating the fruit Sir Licksalot disappears into the rainforest. I follow Sir Licksalot's path of flattened grass. "Sir Licksalot, come here boy."

"Blaze, where are you going?" Danny asks.

"I am going to get Sir Licksalot before he gets lost," I answer.

"We'll come with you. We need to stick together, who knows what else lurks in this forest," Bobby says.

"Big Bad Bobby is scared again," Timmy jokes.

Bobby gives Timmy a dirty look and says, "Keep stuffing your face."

"What's wrong with getting your daily amount of fruit?" Timmy inquires.

"Nothing when it is throughout the day. You do it in one sitting!" Bobby laughs.

"I think I see him over there," I interrupt, pointing towards some plants.

"What is that with him?" Timmy asks.

We quietly sneak in to get a closer look. "It's a goose," Bobby whispers.

I cover Bobby's mouth, and point towards a clump of plants.

Coming out from behind the plants is a family of nene. We see a dad, a mom, and six little babies. The parents are big, the size of Sir Licksalot, or maybe even a little bigger. They look like Canadian geese. Their bodies are black and white, which on some feathers blur into a grey color. They have long tan necks with black jagged designs that reach up to their cheek bones. Their heads are all black. The babies are adorable. They are all brown with a little white on their chests. Their feathers on their necks and heads are fuzzy.

Sir Licksalot, standing next to the male nene, seems to want to smell him. Every time he tries to sniff the goose, the nene opens his wings to flap them and he pushes Sir Licksalot away.

Sir Licksalot gets discouraged and lies down on the ground. The family of nene parade by him. Sir Licksalot's fluffy tail rapidly wags back and forth. I realize that he wants to play with the nene. The family waddles away for about twenty feet, and then we hear a small honk. Sir Licksalot comes to attention, and one more baby nene appears around the bush.

Sir Licksalot moves slowly towards it with a playful goofy stride. The baby flaps his wings and starts honking, which doesn't discourage Sir Licksalot at all. I can tell that he is on a mission to smell that bird. The nene picks up its pace so that it can catch up with its family, which is when Sir Licksalot starts to chase him.

"Sir Licksalot, No!" I yell out.

The adult nenes turn back to retrieve the last youngster, and the rest of the babies follow their parents. Sir Licksalot is now face to face with the baby nene.

I call out to Sir Licksalot over and over again, but nothing is going to break his concentration. Not wanting to scare the nene and give them a heart attack, we remain hidden.

Bobby mumbles, "This is going to get ugly."

The baby nene looks Sir Licksalot in the eye and lets out a small honk. Sir Licksalot lunges towards the nene and opens his mouth. The nene turns its head away in fear, which is when Sir Licksalot starts to lick the nene from the middle of its neck all the way up to the side of its head, giving the goose a big wet kiss. After a while the nene shakes off the slobber. The fuzzy feathers on the side of its head are standing straight up. Sir Licksalot turns towards the other babies and he does the same thing to each one.

Timmy starts laughing. "A goose with a Mohawk!"

Bobby looks at me. "What kind of dog is that? He is supposed to attack birds, not lick them to death."

"He is the one and only Sir Licksalot," I reply smiling at my dog.

CHAPTER 10
The Culture

While I am praising Sir Licksalot for being a good boy, Danny pulls the book out of the pocket in my shorts.

"Let's read some more of this book," Danny suggests.

"Can you walk and read?" Bobby asks.

"Yes. I can walk, talk, and chew gum at the same time too," Danny responds.

"Good. Then we can keep looking for Cici while you read," Bobby says.

Danny flips to the page where Cici left off:

Goddess Pele, not sparing any expense, made a very large home for herself when she created Haleakala. Haleakala means the house by the sun. It is a shield volcano that erupted a million years ago. The crater itself is seven and a half miles long and two and a half miles wide. The coldest it can get at the summit is twelve degrees, and the hottest it has ever been is seventy-three degrees.

Only a few plants can live in the harsh conditions created by the high elevation, lava soil, and wind. Silversword is a plant that is so well adapted to Haleakala that it is found nowhere else in the world. The plants are often several feet tall and the leaves are covered with silvery hairs that help them to retain moisture and reflect the sunlight. The plants produce a hundred or more purple flowers. Silverswords live for fifteen to fifty years. They bloom once and then die.

I interrupt Danny's reading. "That must be the plant Sir Licksalot was digging under when he found the book."

The guys nod in agreement and then Danny continues reading:

Below the crater, there are steep lush mountain slopes where there are rainforests, costal and tropical habitats, and a river that is many miles long. The river cascades down, following the course of an ancient lava flow. Goddess Hina's home is next to this river in a cave under a large waterfall called Rainbow Falls. Inside the cave, there are carvings of Goddess Hina on the lava rock walls. The river continues to cascade through the sacred pools and to the boiling pots. The boiling pots are pools where ancient lava once boiled ferociously and sent steam many, many feet up into the air. Although time has cooled the lava, the boiling pots still bubble and surge with water during heavy rains.

"Boiling pots? Do you think that is a hot spring?" Bobby asks.

Danny hushes Bobby. "Shush. Let me read."

In the forest, you will find at least one thousand native species of flowering plants. Ninety percent of these plants are endemic, found only on the islands. There were one hundred and forty bird species here, but now eighty-five of these species are extinct, and thirty-two remain endangered. Our state bird, the nene, was almost extinct and there were only fifty birds left. Now, thanks to conservation efforts, there are about two hundred and fifty. The forest gets approximately three hundred inches of rain a year. Wild pigs are horrible for the fragile ecosystems. With their big tusks, pointy hooves, and big heavy bodies, the pigs trample the land, disturbing the ground and native plants destroying mosses and ferns. Thankfully, humans are working hard to reduce the pig population by living off the land.

A little further down the mountain there is a jungle of banyan trees, ferns, vines, koa trees, ohi'a, and bamboo that is surrounded by cliffs. There are numerous waterfalls that are fed by the rains. The fog and rain also add to the lush tropical beauty. The red ohi'a flower is sacred. If you pick one, it is said that it will begin to rain hard. The myths reveal that the raindrops are the tears of the Goddesses who weep because humans do not respect nature.

I look at Timmy. "Dude, you upset the Goddesses by picking that flower."

"Come on, do you really believe this stuff?" Bobby asks, in a sarcastic tone of voice.

"Maybe there is something to the myth. Let me finish," Danny replies, and he continues to read:

The closer you get to sea level the easier the journey gets. There are many trees that produce edible fruit including papaya, mango, guava, and coconut. Breathtaking flowers grow here, many of which can be picked as offerings for Aloha. These include many varieties of ilima, lobelias, orchids, protea, pincushion, birds of paradise and, ginger.

"Aloha! I know where we are. We are in Hawaii!" Danny excitedly shares.

"No way," Bobby adds, shaking his head in disbelief.

I chime in, "Way! This all makes sense now, the volcano and the waterfalls. Just look around."

Still eating the last few pieces of fruit Timmy has left in his hands, he mumbles, "Paradise!"

Danny turns the page, and continues to read:

Here on the island the ancient culture still dominates. Each gender has specific activities that they do for fun. The boys mountain surf, fly above the waterfalls, cliff dive, throw spears, make tiki carvings, climb coconut trees, make fires, and design tattoos. The girls create beautiful lei's out of flowers, leaves and sometimes fruit. They weave baskets, make grass skirts, and create hula stories and dances. Both boys and girls enjoy swimming in the natural pools. They also chant and perform hula together during a luau, all under the watchful eye of the Goddesses.

My people are known for our extraordinary friendliness. Our smile and kind warmth invites strangers from all walks of life to become our friends. "Aloha" is the most used word on the islands. It means hello and goodbye, and it implies friendship and love as well as goodwill. It also has a deeper meaning: to share life energy. This energy is the divine power known as "mana." I believe mana is the ultimate secret to a great life. The more mana we create and share, the healthier, happier and successful we will all be.

Looking at Bobby, Timmy says, "Mana up dude!"

Bobby remarks, "You are such a fa…"

"Freaking artistic genius," I interrupt.

Bobby gives me yet another dirty look and folds his fingers into fists.

Danny puts the book down, clenches his fist and does a soft knuckle tap with Bobby's fist. "Mana!"

Bobby shakes his head. "You have all lost your minds." He starts to walk further into the rainforest. "Are you losers coming to help me find my sister?"

"Yeah, wait up!" I shout out. "Come on Sir Licksalot. Let's go find Cici."

We run to catch up with Bobby. Sir Licksalot gently picks up the book and trots after us.

The ground is getting muddier the further we walk. Soon after we notice how slick the surface is, all of us slip, land flat on our backs, and go sliding down a muddy slope.

"Ahhhh!" we all scream.

"Grab anything you can," I yell out.

Bobby screams, "I'm gonna die…"

Again I tell him, "Grab anything. The vines, a tree branch, anything!"

Finally, we all get a hold of something as we dangle on the slope. Sir Licksalot slides in between us flat on his stomach with all four of his legs spread out. He still has the book in his mouth.

"Sir Licksalot!" I scream.

Everyone tries to reach for him, but his wet muddy fur slips right through everyone's hands and he goes sliding down the mountainside.

With tears falling down my cheeks, I use all my strength to climb up the vine that I grabbed to get to a rock ledge.

"He will be ok. After all he is Sir Licksalot," Danny says, trying to reassure me with compassion in his voice.

"I don't think he can survive that fall dude. If he is alive, I'm sure he is badly hurt. His legs were spread out, he probably broke them," I share sniffling.

Everyone looks down, trying to catch a glimpse of him. Nothing. Not even a whimper. We are surrounded by silence except for the slopping of our feet in the mud as we try to climb back up and save ourselves, one wet muddy step at a time.

CHAPTER 11
Girl Bonding

Cici is still cruising down the path learning about all the different flowers from her new friend Alana. Alana is pulling the flowers out of her basket, telling Cici the name of each one.

"When we reach a waterfall, you can wash the dirt off yourself and then I will show you how to make a lei using these flowers," Alana says.

"Seriously?"

"Yes. We will use the flowers and leaves that I already collected."

"I can't wait," Cici says happily.

"Where are you from?" Alana asks Cici.

"California."

"Do you have a lot of friends?" Alana inquires.

"I have two really good friends, Tabitha and Jesse. They are my neighbors. The other girls at school are mean to me though," Cici explains.

"Why?"

"I don't know. They tease me, and they don't even know me. One girl calls me a bleach blonde twig," Cici says sadly. "I think they hate me. They push my stuff out of my hands and laugh at me when I have to get down on the floor to pick everything up. Sometimes they trip me up when I am walking in the hallways at school. The last time I was tripped, I was eating a cupcake. When I pulled myself up off the ground, everyone was laughing because I had frosting all over my face. I was so embarrassed."

Alana stares at Cici with a horrified look on her face.

"They all think my brother Bobby is the hottest guy in school, so when he is around they act totally different towards me, all fake and chummy. My brother knows what they are really like and that they treat me badly. He doesn't give them the time of day," Cici continues.

"Goddess Hina watches over children," Alana says, trying to reassure Cici.

"I don't think she watches over me much. Why can't a person just be himself or herself without someone picking on him or her? No one is nice to me. Most of them make fun of my freckles, while others say I am too skinny. When I look in the mirror, the only reflection I see is their opinion of me. Why are girls so mean?" Cici asks.

"They are just jealous," Alana says.

Cici bends her head down. "I don't think so. Look at me! Who would be jealous of this?"

"Maybe they weren't taught how to respect others," Alana suggests. "I was taught to respect every living thing including bugs and animals, plants and fruit, the land, and the people that live on it."

"I don't think people care about anyone's feelings, but their own. As for respect, well I don't think most of the people I have met even know what that word means. Many people definitely don't care about the land. People litter all the time. You see some adults picking up after the kids, and other adults contributing to the mess. The girls I know only care about what brand of clothes they are wearing, who their BFF is, what dreamy guy they want to be with, taking pictures of themselves, and of course, gossip!"

"BFF?" Alana asks with a puzzled look on her face.

"It means best friends forever. In reality it means best friends for now until the next girl comes along and takes your place," Cici explains.

"You will always be my friend," Alana says.

Cici hugs Alana. "I am so glad we met. You are so different from anyone I have ever met. You are so pure and naturally beautiful. Even if I put a lot of make up on I still wouldn't look as pretty as you do."

Clearly embarrassed, Alana responds by saying, "Mahalo. You don't need to cover up your face with make up. You are perfect just the way you are."

Cici smiles and then says, "I wish everyone was like you. Thank you, Alana. You are the best birthday gift ever."

Alana tilts her head and listens intently. "Do you hear that?"

"No."

"Listen, you can hear the running water. We are near," Alana says.

Not in tune with the land the way Alana is, Cici still doesn't hear it. The girls walk a little faster, eager to reach the water. Cici trips and loses her shoes in the sugarcane field. Noticing Alana is barefoot she continues on without searching for them.

When they arrive at a pool that lies beneath a waterfall, Cici runs and jumps in. Alana sits next to the pool and begins to sort the flowers in her basket.

"Come on. Come in and play," Cici says trying to encourage Alana to join her in the water.

"I can't. I have work to do. I must make all the leis for the luau and practice my hula before dusk," Alana replies.

"But I will help you. We will get the same amount done in half the time. That gives you a few minutes to play in the water and plenty of time to perfect your hula dance. Please," Cici begs.

"I can't," Alana says again.

"Will you teach me how to hula?" Cici asks.

"I will teach you the hula that will be performed tonight," Alana says, gently smiling.

Cici swims over to the side of the pool and uses the rocks to step out. She takes her long blonde hair into her hands and wrings out the water. Her purple tank top stretches down to her blue jean cut-offs as the fresh water drips from both. Walking over to Alana, she sits down beside her to learn how to make leis.

Alana begins to teach Cici. "It's really easy. You just have to be careful not to break the delicate flowers when you thread them together. You will use this needle, which is about ten inches long, and this string, which is about forty-five inches long. Thread the string through the needle and then carefully put the flowers onto the string by placing the needle directly in the center of the flower from front to back. Once the needle has three or more flowers on it, gently slide the flowers down onto the string. You can mix the flowers if you want to, or you can make the whole lei with the same flowers. At least one yellow ilima flower needs to be included on each lei because it is sacred to Laka, Goddess of the Hula. Be very careful though because these flowers are so thin; they are as fragile as tissue paper."

After what seems like a really long time spent on stringing flowers, Cici ties the ends of her lei together. "I finished one. I can't believe I made something so beautiful," she says with delight.

"Why would you think that you couldn't make it?" Alana asks with surprise.

"Because everything I touch turns out badly," Cici says.

"Believe in yourself, you have Mana," Alana says.

"Mana?"

"Life energy."

Cici looks at Alana oddly.

"Mana means divine power."

Cici places her first lei around Alana's neck and whispers in her ear, "Aloha."

"Mahalo," Alana replies.

Alana reaches over to the green ferns and small leaves and says, "I will now teach you how to make a head piece. Take some fern, leaves, and a couple of the small white flowers. Place the fern and leaves in a circle making a base. Use the twine to wrap the ferns and leaves together. Continue adding ferns and leaves to the base until it is layered like this. You will do the same thing to make a lei for your brother. Using the Ti leaves weave or braid the leaves together, like this."

Cici is amazed to see how Alana uses the plants and materials from the forest to make these traditional yet beautiful accessories. Under a canopy of trees, the girls continue to work hard making the leis for the luau.

CHAPTER 12
Living Native

Slipping and sliding in the mud, Timmy, Danny, Bobby and I make our way over to a rock ledge. We have two options. One is to continue up the muddy slope. The second is to slide down a horizontal vine. I start to pull my shirt off and Bobby asks, "Blaze, what the heck are you doing?"

"I'm going to wrap my shirt over the vine and hold on to my shirt as I slide down the vine."

"Sick! I'm in," Timmy says pulling his shirt up over his head.

"I wish I'd thought of that," Danny says, eager to participate.

"Count me out! I am not going. No way. No how!" Bobby says crossing his arms.

"Bobby, it's the only practical way down," Danny says, trying to convince him to go along.

Bobby puts his hands over his mouth. "I'm going to be sick."

"Get over it. Take your shirt off and let's go. Think of it as flying through the jungle," Timmy tells Bobby.

Making throw up sounds and motions, Bobby shakes his head.

"It's your choice. You can stay here forever, or you can have a little faith. The vine is sturdy," I say. "See," and I pull on the vine to show him how strong it is.

"Who's going first?" Danny asks.

Timmy already has his shirt wrapped around the vine and without waiting, he jumps off the ledge. As he slides down, he sings a verse from '*Free Fallin'*.

Danny follows immediately after him. "Yippe ki yay!"

I look at Bobby. "It's now or never."

"I can't. You know I am afraid of heights. It is a long, long way down if I fall off," Bobby says. I can see that he is really scared.

"The only way you would fall is if you let go."

"I would never let go. I am not weak," Bobby says angrily.

"Prove it," I say.

Bobby pulls his shirt off and wraps it around the vine, and before he can think about what he is doing, I push him off the ledge. Bobby is screaming at the top of his lungs as he goes sliding down the vine. "I will get you Blaze!"

I wrap my shirt around the vine and jump off, trailing just behind Bobby.

"This is so sick!" Timmy shouts.

"Check out the waterfall on the left. It has to be at least four hundred feet tall," Danny yells out.

Bobby's eyes are tightly closed shut. I, on the other hand, am enjoying the ride, though I look all around hoping to see Sir Licksalot praying he made it down the muddy slope safely.

Timmy comes to the end of our jungle made zip line, and he jumps down into the bamboo forest. Danny follows after him. Bobby doesn't know he is at the end because he won't open his eyes.

"Bobby, open your eyes you are at the end," Timmy warns him.

"No way!" Bobby shouts out.

Bobby hits a moss-covered tree and falls down to the ground, landing on top of Timmy and Danny. I get to the end and I see that there is a small waterfall nearby. I jump down. "I found water," I wave my hand. "Follow me."

"I hope we can drink the water," Timmy says.

"Of course we can. Moving river water is usually clean," Danny shares.

The sound of rushing water is getting nearer and nearer with every step I make. I can't wait to get rinsed off and to get a drink. When I get to the river, I see that I am going to have to walk on some wet slippery rocks. I take it very, very slowly. The water in the river is raging, and the force of the water could pull me in. The waterfall is only a few feet downstream. I ask Danny to hold onto my leg while I lie down on a rock to get a drink of water. The water is so refreshing and it tastes so pure. I cup my hand and splash water over my very dirty body and hair. Danny and Timmy take a turn too. Bobby is standing a few feet away pouting as usual.

I walk over to Bobby and tell him, "Get some water dude."

"No thanks," Bobby responds.

"Why?"

"Do you see how far that water drops down the waterfall? I get dizzy just thinking about it," Bobby confesses.

Feeling badly for Bobby, I tell him that I will get him some water.

Trying to figure out what to put the water in so that he can get a decent drink, I trudge through the bamboo forest and, guess who I see chewing on a dried up piece of bamboo? "I can't believe it. Sir Licksalot, you are okay!"

Sir Licksalot is lying down wagging his tail. I begin to worry wondering why he won't get up. My heart starts pounding as panic sets in. Did he break his leg? As I am kneeling down to check on him, Sir Licksalot jumps up and gives me a big wet juicy kiss. Tears of relief that he is not hurt fill my eyes. Petting Sir Licksalot, I look at where he was lying. He was lying over the book, protecting it. I put the book in my back pocket and continue to rub his belly, "You are unbelievably lucky boy! I don't know how you do it. You must have some serious mana!"

Sir Licksalot keeps licking me, and I remember that I need to find something for Bobby to drink out of. Next to Sir Licksalot's bamboo stick there is the remainder of what was once a bamboo trunk. I break a curved section off and run back towards the guys, calling out to Sir Licksalot as I leave. "Come on boy!"

Sir Licksalot grabs his bamboo stick as if it is a bone and trots after me.

Reaching Bobby, I tell him, "Check it out. I found this. We can use it as a bowl to get some water for you to drink."

Bobby's eyes get brighter. Danny holds my leg, and after I fill up the bamboo bowl I pass it to Danny. Danny passes it to Timmy, and Timmy walks it over to Bobby. We continue the assembly line until Bobby feels replenished and refreshed. With the last bowl of the water in his hands, Timmy walks over to Bobby and Bobby puts his hands out. With a smirk on his face, Timmy looks over at us, winks, and pours the water over Bobby's head, giving him a shower. Bobby jumps up and chases Timmy into the bamboo forest shouting out, "Just wait until I catch you!"

CHAPTER 13
Hula

As the girls continue making accessories for the luau, Cici learns about the spirituality of the hula.

Alana provides Cici with some background. "Hula is the soul of Hawaii. In ancient times, hula is considered a spiritual ritual dance that is performed for the Gods and Goddesses who aid the mortals. Today, it is a form of entertainment, often portraying a romantic story. Every move and expression the dancer makes is significant. The dancer may be representing a flower, an animal, waves, or even the wind."

"Do you still dance for the Goddesses?" Cici asks.

"If we are not putting on a show for visitors, we dance for the Goddesses. This brings about more life energy, more mana." Alana confirms. "The Hula Kahiko is an ancient hula dance that requires strength and agility. This hula will be performed at the luau tonight. Dancers will use pahu, which are drums of various sizes. The drums can be made of coconut shells or tree trunks. You and I will use the ili'ili.' They are small water-worn pebbles. When they are clicked together, they make a rhythmic sound. Where the river meets the ocean we will look for two stones that will fit perfectly in your hands."

"When can I get my ili'ili'?" Cici asks, interrupting Alana.

"As soon as we finish the leis and I teach you the mele. A mele is a chant. I will teach you using our native words."

"Got it."

"The mele for tonight is called He Mea Nani Nō. which means 'Beautiful Purpose.' I created it myself. Are you ready to repeat after me?" Alana asks.

"Yep," Cici says excitedly.

Alana: **Mālama `o Hina i nā mea a pau loa mai luna mai o ka mahina**
Cici: **Mālama `o Hina i nā mea a pau loa mai luna mai o ka mahina**
Alana: **Hō`omo`omo `o Pele i ka honua**
Cici: **Hō`omo`omo `o Pele i ka honua**
Alana: **Ho`ohanohano `o Laka i nā mea a pau loa**
Cici: **Ho`ohanohano `o Laka i nā mea a pau loa**
Alana: **He mea ho`ākua nō kēia**
Cici: **He mea ho`ākua nō kēia**
Alana: **He mana nō ke aloha ā pilialoha**
Cici: **He mana nō ke aloha ā pilialoha**
Alana: **Loa`a `ia i ka nani o Haleakalā**
Cici: **Loa`a `ia i ka nani o Haleakalā**
Alana: **I kēlā wahi wau i a`o `ia ai e pili ana ia'u**
Cici: **I kēlā wahi wau i a`o `ia ai e pili ana ia'u**
Alana: **Mai ka huaka`i i ke kai**
Cici: **Mai ka huaka`i i ke kai**

"Not bad for your first time using the native tongue, Cici. We will practice all day. Let me share the English version with you so that the words mean something to you."

Hina protects from the moon
Pele shapes the earth
Laka honors nature of all kind
People consider all of this divine
Love and friendship form mana
found on beautiful Haleakala
where I learned about me
along the journey to the sea

"You are so talented Alana. I really like it," Cici says, with sparkling eyes.

As they make the remaining leis, Cici continues to practice the mele in Hawaiian, following Alana's lead.

CHAPTER 14
Traditional Extreme Sports

Still dripping wet from head to toe, Sir Licksalot, Danny, and I chase Bobby who is still trying to find Timmy in the bamboo forest.

"You are dead meat when I find you," Bobby yells out.

After a lot of running around, we finally catch up with Bobby. Sir Licksalot is sniffing and licking a piece of fallen wood.

"Stop that. You are going to get sick," I tell Sir Licksalot.

"Timmy was just playing around," Danny tells Bobby.

"No. He was trying to make me look like an idiot," Bobby says, with a scowl on his face.

"You do that all by yourself," I say, unable to resist the temptation.

"Throwing your muscle around, and using mean words doesn't impress us," Danny adds.

"What are you talking about?" Bobby asks.

"You are always trying to be so big and bad, that you don't even consider our feelings when you say the things you do. Now Timmy is missing and it's your fault because you wanted to beat him up for pouring water on you," Danny explains. "What's your problem?"

"Hey, I have an idea. Seriously! Try giving respect to receive respect!" I add. "You don't beat respect out of people you simply earn it by being considerate to other people."

"I don't even know who I am anymore. I have this image of what I should be, and I don't know how to get rid of it. I know when we get into middle school it's only going to get worse," Bobby explains, looking miserable.

"I am afraid to go to middle school too," I say, in a subtle voice.

"You are afraid! Bobby says. Try being me! Before fifth grade ended, everyone that I ever had a problem with wrote in my yearbook that they will meet up with me in middle school with their older and stronger friends."

"I'll have your back, if you'll have mine," I offer.

"Ditto." Danny chimes in.

"What are you going to do Danny, stun them with your idiotic gadgets?" Bobby asks.

"Hey, we just said that we would watch your back in middle school. Why do you always have to say something rude? We are trying to be your friends," I remark.

"I guess I feel I have to keep up the image," Bobby mumbles.

Just then Timmy appears from under a piece of wood saying, "All this time I have thought that one day you were going to snap and actually kill me. Now I find out that all you have been doing is practicing to protect an image you don't even like?"

"What can I say?" Bobby replies.

"How about, I am sorry. Or, I didn't mean any of it," Danny says.

"I am sorry. Okay, are you happy?"

"That is not at all sincere," Danny replies.

Timmy says, "He won't apologize properly when he thinks he hasn't done anything wrong." Timmy turns away in disgust and places his foot on the piece the wood that he was hiding under, and in a flash Timmy is riding it like a sled down a long trench covered in grass. Timmy manages to control the fast ride yelling out, "This is sweet. I am surfing the mountain."

Danny starts looking around the forest for more sled-shaped pieces of wood, and when he finds some he hands them to us. "Here take one."

Bobby grabs one first and follows Timmy down. I follow shortly after, sitting on the wood sled with Sir Licksalot sitting between my legs. Danny pulls out his GPS to find our coordinates and then he too hops on a sled. Flying down the hill at great speeds brings laughter and fun back. We eventually arrive at the base of the trench where there is a hillside covered with lava rocks.

"Now what?" Bobby asks.

"We surf the rock," Timmy states.

"Are you crazy?" Bobby inquires.

"A real warrior would do it," Timmy says, taunting Bobby's false image.

"I'm going. Who is with me?" Timmy asks.

"I'm in," Danny answers.

"Us too," I answer.

We all give Bobby the look.

Danny pulls the book out of his back pocket and hands it to Bobby telling him, "You can choose to join us or you can sit here and read."

"Read. Are you serious? I don't read unless I have to for school," Bobby says, handing the book to me.

Putting the book into my pocket, I respond to his comment. "That explains a lot."

Tired of waiting, Timmy picks up his sled, and walks over to the top of the lava rock hill. He lays his sled down, puts his ear buds in and with a soft push, as if to start a skateboard, Timmy maneuvers his way down the hill. This has to be the most dangerous stunt any of us have ever tried. Needing to salvage a little of his pride, Bobby gets ready to go next, and Danny follows him. I have a little dilemma, and his name is Sir Licksalot. There is no way I can surf a rocky hill with him on my sled. Sitting at the top of the slope, I contemplate what I should do. The guys are close to the bottom already and I can just hear the faint echoes of their chatter. I scope out our surroundings and find what resembles an old basket. I find some extremely strong leaves beneath the trees, ones that I can't even break, and weave them into the sides of the basket. I put my right arm under one of the leaves and then I place my left arm under the other leaf, effectively making a backpack. Kneeling down, I call out to Sir Licksalot, "Come boy. Get in."

Sir Licksalot hesitates, but with a little more encouragement, he finally jumps in. I straighten my sled and jump on. Soon I am flying along at what feels like at least fifty miles an hour down a steep and incredibly bumpy hill. The breeze generated by the speed of the descent dries my hair and my clothes by the time Sir Licksalot and I reach the bottom.

"Dude, what took so long?" Timmy asks, lying on the ground resting.

Bending down to let Sir Licksalot out of the homemade backpack, I show the guys what I found. "I found this basket and made this backpack thing so that I could get Sir Licksalot down the hill."

"Now that is genius," Danny says, giving me a pat on the back.

"Why are you guys wet?" I ask.

Pointing over the ledge Bobby explains. "We got tired of waiting for your butt so we went swimming."

Just below us is a very small waterfall and pool with my name written all over it. I take the book out of my pocket and put it in a dry place, and then I dive in and begin to swim around. Danny and Timmy jump in and we start to goof off, dunking each other. Bobby soon dives in to join us, and I begin to hope that maybe we are getting through to him at last. Sir Licksalot isn't interested in swimming, and he waits for us on the rocks. Pulling myself up out of the water, I notice that some water is spilling over the edge of the pool. I hold onto the edge and inch my way over to see where the water is going. The force of the water current pushes me so hard that my hands slip and in a few moments I am free falling down a waterfall into another pool of water. Once I am able to breathe again, I yell up to the guys. "I'm down here."

I hear Timmy talking to the others. "Did you hear something?" he says.

"I'm down here," I shout again.

"Down where?" Timmy asks.

"Go to the edge and look down," I tell him.

Danny swims to the edge and pulls himself up with his arms so that he can balance on his waist. He looks over. "How did you get down there?"

"I went down the waterfall. Hey, check it out. There are natural steps in the rock that you can use to climb down. We can cliff dive," I say, pointing to the walls of rock on both sides of the waterfall.

Timmy and Bobby join Danny to see what we are talking about.

"Sounds like fun to me," says Timmy, and he climbs down the side of the rock to a level he is comfortable with. Danny follows him and Bobby stays at the edge of the pool.

"Come on Bobby," Danny calls out.

"That's okay. You guys go. I will stay here with Sir Licksalot and the dumb book," Bobby replies, with his heart beating incredibly fast.

Timmy jumps in from about twenty feet up and does a cannon ball. Danny comes down a little lower to about fifteen feet and then he dives in. Sir Licksalot becomes curious and he finds his way down through the forest and over to us. Now Bobby is all alone.

"Hey. How did he get down there?" Bobby shouts out.

"If we can do it and the dog can do it, you can too. It's time to face your greatest fear and defeat it," Danny yells out.

"Great! Now you sound like the dumb book," Bobby says.

"Just let the water take you down the waterfall," I suggest.

"If you don't come down, I will climb up there and push you over the edge myself!" Danny yells. I can tell that he is starting to get fed up.

"Any day now," Timmy taunts Bobby.

Bobby chickens out. He gets out of the pool, picks up the book, and follows Sir Licksalot's path down to where we are. While Bobby maneuvers his way down, we climb out of the pool and climb back up the rock wall. Each of us goes to a different elevation, and I am at the highest level, at about thirty feet.

"One... Two... Three!"

We all do different tricks in the air, creating a massive cannonball splash that drenches Bobby.

Timmy gets out of the pool to climb back up, which is when he notices that his ear buds are hanging out of his pocket. Reaching for his iPod he has a look of fear on his face.

"What's up Timmy?" I ask.

"My iPod! I forgot I had it in my pocket. And now it's gone!" Timmy says, looking panicky.

I dive down to see if I can see the iPod on the bottom of the pool. Coming back up for air I tell Timmy, "It's too deep. I can't even touch the bottom or see it."

"Just great! My parents are going to kill me!" Timmy says miserably. "And I can't live without music!"

"Party's over," says Bobby, looking just a little smug.

Getting out of the pool, we shake the water out of our ears and our hair. Bobby hands me the book. "You carry this."

I take the book and put it in my pocket. Bobby then leads the way through the rainforest, closely following the river. We walk single file through the moss, ferns, and trees. Danny pulls out his GPS to see exactly where we are.

"We are at five thousand feet. We are halfway to the bottom," Danny says excitedly. A few moments pass and then Danny blurts out saying, "I know what I am going to do when I grow up. I am going to become an entrepreneur of electronic ingenuity or a tour guide. Or maybe even both."

"That sounds like you. I think that I am meant to be a professional basketball player," I share.

"My future is a slam dunk too. I'm going to be an entertainer!" Timmy adds.

"No doubt about that," Danny remarks.

Bobby keeps walking and he doesn't say anything.

"Dude, what about you?" Timmy asks Bobby.

"I don't know. The only thing I am really good at is lifting weights and protecting my little sisters," Bobby mumbles.

"Despite the fact that you have a reputation of being a bully, you are very protective of your sisters. With your strength you could become a body guard," I suggest.

"Maybe. What about a fire fighter? I've thought about that many times. I can carry people out of a burning building or move heavy objects that fall on people. My fear of heights is a concern though. The thought of climbing a ladder makes me ill," Bobby says.

"See Bobby, you aren't a bully. It's just an image to hide behind. I admire you for wanting to help people in dangerous situations."

"Really?"

"If you spent more time being yourself, rather than trying to be someone you aren't, you would be a much happier person and way more fun to be around," Danny says.

Bobby looks happy when he hears this, and I even see a little smile creep across his face. Maybe we are really getting through to him at last.

Just then something catches Sir Licksalot's attention and he runs ahead towards the river. By the time we reach the river, Sir Licksalot is standing on some rocks poking his nose in and out of the water as it breaks over the rocks. Quietly walking up to see what the dog is interested in, we see tons of fish. There are tiny yellow fish, green fish, half black and half orange fish, even silver ones with a purple-blue outline. The fish range in size from a few inches to about a foot long. Sir Licksalot is having the time of his life as the fish swim down the river and under his skinny long pink tongue as he tries to lick them as they pass.

CHAPTER 15
Mana

Taking a breather from all the excitement of our 'extreme sports events,' we gather under the tropical trees while Sir Licksalot plays with the fish in the river. We all rest our backs against a tree trunk. I can't quite get comfortable though because something is poking me. Reaching underneath to move whatever it is that I am sitting on, I realize that it's not a stick or a rock, it's the book. I forgot that Bobby gave me the book. Pulling it out of my pocket, I ask everyone, "Want me to read the end of the story now?"

"No time like the present," Danny answers.

I flip through the pages to find the place where Danny left off.

We create mana in many ways. One way is through hula. Hula is a spiritual dance honoring the Gods and Goddesses. It tells a story using motions that imitate human actions and things in nature. For instance, the motion for picking a flower is to place your arms straight out with palms facing outward. Turn your hands in and allow your fingers to touch your palms as though you are holding a flower. Rain is considered a gift from nature as it blesses the land allowing all things to grow, and it is often described in hula dances. The motion for rain is to reach your hands up to the side of your body and wiggle your fingers and then sweep your hands down to your waist. Movements at your waist represent sea level, everything above the waist represents everything over the land, and everything below the waist represents all that is under water. There are many motions, including expressions on the face, which are used in Hula.

Mele is a chant that is a part of the hula. It is an essential part of the story, and it is always performed with emotion.

The dancers wear costumes made from things that grow on the land. Women wear grass skirts made of Ti leaves and men wear leis made from ferns and leaves on their wrists and ankles. They also wear a kapa loin cloth made from the bark of a tree. Since the forest and plants are an element of Laka, Goddess of the Hula, the sacred hula ritual is considered a form of the Goddess herself, who shares her mana with all who attend the hula.

"This is chick stuff. Do we have to hear anymore?" Bobby says, looking impatient.

"I think it is kind of interesting to learn about another culture's traditions," Danny says.

"Of course you would. You are a …"

I stop Bobby in his tracks. "Don't call him a name just because he is interested in something other than himself."

"Something? Last I heard you were going on about mana. How lame is that?" Bobby bites back.

"Ignore him and continue," Danny says.

Bobby folds his arms in frustration and I continue to read:

The ancient hand-carved wooden figures, known as tiki, represent the spiritual powers of the gods and goddesses. Mortals believe they can get mana from the tiki, but only a few people have the skill to carve a tiki.

Some mortals use black ink to make body art known as tattoos. The ink is made from burned kukui nut soot mixed with juice from coconuts and sugarcane. Tattoos are allowed under specific spiritual rules, and the designs have hidden meaning and spiritual power. Mortals wear the tattoos with pride knowing that they have a connection with divine power.

Danny stops me. "Hang on Blaze."

"Explain to me what is so lame about learning about Hawaiian tattoos," Danny asks Bobby.

"Okay that was interesting," Bobby admits.

Danny smiles and then tells me to continue reading.

I flip the page and start to read:

It is my belief that the gods and goddesses, and the land and the mortals are interconnected. If the mortals don't mistreat the land but take care of it, the goddesses will bless the land by providing an abundance of resources.

I close the book and lay it on the ground, "That's it. It stops there."

"I now realize why the Hawaiians treat the earth and all living things with so much respect. It's a shame that all people aren't as respectful. The earth would be a much kinder and cleaner place if we all followed their example," Danny says, looking thoughtful.

"Can we do a guy thing now?" Bobby asks.

"What do you have in mind?" I ask.

"How about pretending that you are the dart board and I throw these bamboo sticks at you," Bobby responds.

"Oh nice, Bobby!" Danny comments.

"Sure," I respond.

"I'm joking," Bobby says.

"I'm not. Come on," I say, getting up from the ground. "Whoever catches the most bamboo spears will win."

Danny says, "Isn't that dangerous?"

"If he wants to act like a warrior then he needs to prove he is one," I say, looking around for bamboo poles to make spears.

"When did this turn into a competition?" Bobby inquires.

"You are always looking for attention. Now you have it. All eyes will be on you," I respond.

"Fine. Bring it on!" Bobby shouts out as he gets up.

Timmy brings over a perfect piece of bamboo to make a spear out of and then sits down next to the book. I take the bamboo stick and walk back over to the river where Sir Licksalot is still trying to catch a fish and I rub it hard against a rock, making the point very, very sharp. Sir Licksalot comes over to see what I am doing. Frustrated with Bobby I tell Sir Licksalot, "I'm going to have to teach that Bobby Cooper a lesson, once and for all."

"What's taking so long?" Bobby hollers out.

"I'm coming!" I shout back. Under my breath I mumble, "If anything will open his eyes, this will."

I tread back to the spot where the guys are. Sir Licksalot follows closely behind me. Danny and Timmy are sitting next to each other. Timmy has the book in his lap and he is tapping a beat on it. Bobby takes position about twenty feet away from me. He pounds his chest and says, "Show me what you got!"

I place my hand down on the lower portion of the spear, pull my arm back, and throw it as hard as I can, straight at Bobby. Bobby dodges it by jumping out of the way.

Bobby walks over to pick up the spear. "I wasn't ready yet."

"Whatever you say, Bobby," I respond.

Bobby prepares to throw the spear at me. He throws it hard and it whips by my left side. With my right hand I pull the spear out of the air. The guys sit in silence while Sir Licksalot whimpers.

"Are you ready this time?" I ask.

"Yep," Bobby answers.

Again I throw the spear as hard as I can and Bobby tries to catch it and misses.

"That's one for Blaze N. Haught and zero for Bobby Cooper," Timmy calls out.

Bobby picks up the spear and chucks it at me. I lower to my knees and still manage to catch it. Standing up, I reach back and throw the spear with all my might. Bobby misses it.

"That's two for Blaze N. Haught and zero for Bobby Cooper," Timmy calls out.

Distraught, Bobby finally gives up. "Fine. You win."

"You are giving up already?" I ask.

"I can't do this. What is the point of going on? I'm going to get killed."

"I only did it to show you that if you keep provoking people, one day someone is going to take you up on your threats. The next time you might end up getting really hurt by someone who has a real weapon. "

"He is right Bobby," Danny agrees.

"You just need to mana up, dude!" Timmy tells Bobby.

Bobby shakes his head and rolls his eyes.

"Don't dismiss it, there is something to it," I add.

"Says who?" Bobby asks.

Timmy quickly answers showing Bobby the book. "The people who believe in the myths written in this book."

"And the person who wrote the book too," Danny adds.

"Okay. I give. I give." Bobby says looking defeated yet again. "We need to keep going and look for Cici."

"Can we find some more food too? I'm a growing boy," Timmy asks.

"Sure," Bobby says, not even trying to protest this time.

Timmy jumps up and takes off to look for food. We trail just behind him. Sir Licksalot notices that Timmy left the book behind so he picks it up gently with his teeth and trots over to join us.

CHAPTER 16
Coconut Anyone

Danny consults his GPS as we parade through the forest following the route he suggested. "We have reached two thousand feet above sea level. We are very close to the bottom now." Danny takes the lead and we follow him as he leads us away from the river.

"Why are we leaving the river?" Bobby asks.

"We need to go southwest now," Danny answers.

"Why?" Bobby asks.

"Because that is the way it shows we are supposed to go," Danny explains, waving the GPS device at him.

"Maybe we should have taken the other path through the wilderness. I'll bet you that is the way Cici went," Bobby says. "It's time we split up now."

"Could be," Danny agrees. "Either way, we will end up at the bottom of the mountain. There are only two paths to get down and it looks like they both connect where the river meets the ocean."

"What if Cici isn't there when we get there?" Bobby asks.

"Then we will all go back to find her. It's not a good idea to split up like the original plan," I share. "Let's keep going. We aren't that far away from the bottom."

Traveling down the mountain, we suddenly find ourselves surrounded by an abundance of lush tropical plants. Thousands of colorful blooms are mixed in with forest greens. My favorite plant looks like my mom's pincushion. It is an orange-yellow ball with orange spider-like legs that have red tips. There are also some flowers that look like birds and others that look like feathers.

Timmy finds a flower that makes him feel even hungrier. "Check it out. When these green and yellow flower buds with the black tips are closed, they are shaped like artichokes and are the color of a pineapple delight."

"Those are called minks," Danny says.

"Dude, you are a walking encyclopedia," Timmy says in amazement.

Sir Licksalot drops the book and wanders through the plants smelling each and every one. The flower petals dance in the air and tickle his nose.

Still in a hurry to find something to eat, Timmy turns and calls out to Sir Licksalot who has a collection of flower petals stuck to his long fluffy tail, "Come on flower boy."

Sir Licksalot stubbornly refuses to come.

"What now?" Bobby asks.

"I don't know. I will get him," I say and I turn back towards the dog.

The guys sit down under a palm tree while I walk back through the flowers to retrieve Sir Licksalot. Sir Licksalot is frantically searching for something. "What is it boy?" I say. "What are you looking for?" Then I spotted the book leaning against the Ohi'a tree. I pick it up. "Is this what you are looking for?"

Sir Licksalot starts barking. I hand him the book and he grips it delicately in his teeth. I don't understand why he is so attached to this book.

The guys are under the palm tree leaning against the trunk. Sir Licksalot runs up to Bobby and jumps on his lap, pushing Bobby's body into the tree. This shakes the tree a little and causes a palm leaf to float down. Looking up into the sky to see where it fell from, Timmy notices something in the tree. With excitement in is eyes and voice he says, "Nuts! It's a giant nut tree."

We all look up into the tree and see some clusters of large round tan colored nuts that are nestled up in the leaves.

"Coconuts you mean," I say.

"I have to have one," Timmy says, staring at the coconuts with mesmerized eyes. "How are we going to get one?"

Bobby shakes the tree. Nothing falls.

"You have to climb the tree," Danny says.

"How?" Timmy asks.

"Put your hands around the tree and place one foot in front of the other so that you can walk up the tree," Danny explains.

Timmy wraps his hands around the tree trunk and starts to climb up. After a few feet, Timmy comes sliding down, scrapping up his arms on the rough tree trunk. Timmy tries it again but he just can't make it up the tree.

"How do they do this?" Timmy asks in frustration.

"I think you have to be barefoot," I suggest. "Let me try."

I take my shoes off and start to climb up the tree. I make it a little farther than Timmy did, but then I have to stop because my feet are getting sore and they hurt. I come back down, very slowly. Timmy looks at Danny.

"There's no way. I don't have any upper body strength," Danny explains.

We all look at Bobby.

"Me?" Bobby asks.

"You have the strength and the agility," I say.

"Okay, but I'm only trying one time," Bobby says, trying not to look pleased about my compliment.

Bobby pulls his shoes off. We all cover our noses and start to feel queasy. Bobby looks over at us. "What's your problem?"

"Dude, your feet hecka stink!" I explain.

"I wouldn't talk. When is the last time you put deodorant on those pits?" Bobby asks.

"I have the best hygiene of everyone," I respond.

"That's only because you haven't reached puberty. You're such a twerp," Bobby states.

"You're just jealous that I am a Totally Wicked, Extraordinarily Responsible Person," I respond.

"Extra what?" Bobby mumbles under his breath.

"For your limited vocabulary, extraordinary means very," Danny says.

Bobby gives us a dirty look as he starts to climb up the tree. He climbs it very quickly and soon he reaches the bottom of the palms.

"Hold on to the fresh strong green leaves. Don't hold on to the brown ones or you will fall," Danny yells up.

Bobby takes his time finding some sturdy leaves to hold on to. Once he finds what he is looking for he shouts down to us. "Now what?"

"Use one hand to hold on, and use the other hand to twist the coconut until it breaks off," Danny explains.

Bobby twists and turns and nothing happens. He yells down, "It won't come off."

"Maybe it isn't ripe," I yell up. "Try another one in a different cluster."

Bobby goes up a little higher in the tree. He is at least thirty feet in the air.

"Just don't look down," Danny jokes.

Bobby's fear of heights is being tested. "I already did, don't remind me."

Bobby reaches the next cluster and he starts to twist a coconut. These coconuts are a little darker in color. Pulling and twisting hard, Bobby manages to loosen some of the nuts and five drop down at the same time.

"You did it Bobby!" Timmy shouts up.

Bobby climbs down just as fast as he climbed up.

"You're a natural," Danny says, grinning at Bobby.

"Piece of cake," Bobby says, wiping off his feet and hands.

Timmy walks up to Bobby and shakes his hand. "Thanks man!"

"I feel good. I faced my fear and I got you something to eat," Bobby says, smiling shyly.

"Now we need to open them," Danny points out. "We need to hit them with something."

We all look around to find something heavy and hard. Sir Licksalot is sitting right next to a rock that looks just right. Picking up the rock, I hand it to Bobby. "You can have the honor."

Bobby smiles and Danny moves the darker coconut over so the seam is facing upwards. Bobby uses all his strength and hits the coconut right in the middle. Juice squirts out hitting Sir Licksalot in the face and on his front legs. We all get a piece of the coconut and sit down to eat it.

Sir Licksalot sits next to me licking the juice off his legs.

Bobby punctures the top of the lighter colored younger coconuts so we can drink the water like juice. Then he breaks open the remaining ripe coconuts for us.

"It seems a shame to throw these shells away," Danny says, as we finish up our snack.

"Throw them away? No way. These will make sick drums. Listen," Timmy says, as he starts to beat the palm of his hands on the coconut shells.

"We need to get moving," Bobby reminds us, shouting over Timmy's noise so that he can be heard.

Timmy starts stacking the shells one inside the other while Danny reviews our coordinates. Sir Licksalot locates his book and Bobby and I put our shoes back on.

"We need to navigate through the sugarcane," Danny states.

"I told you we should have stayed by the river," Bobby grumbles.

Danny takes a deep breath and keeps his cool. "The trail follows the river once we get there. Come on."

CHAPTER 17
Believe

Arriving at the river, Sir Licksalot vanishes. I search high and low for him in the sugarcane field while Timmy, Danny, and Bobby look for him near the river. Where could he possibly be? Did he go into the water and get swept away by in the current? Did he go back into the rainforest? Where is he?

Danny notices a shoe. "Hey, Bobby, look!"

Bobby looks at the ground where Danny is pointing. "It's Cici's shoe!"

Echoes of Sir Licksalot and Cici's names rumble inside my chest, as we all call out their names, one after the other in hopes that we will find them.

Eventually, I make my way back to the river and join the others. Even though we searched and called out for both of them, none us saw any sign of Cici or Sir Licksalot. I sit down on a rock and put my head down between my knees. Danny rubs my back. "I'm sure he's fine. He made it all the way down the mountain. He will find his way through this last stretch too."

Bobby is distraught. Placing his hands on his head he starts to sob.

Timmy starts sniffing the air. "Do you smell that?"

"Now is not a good time to be thinking about your stomach," says Bobby.

"I'm serious. Smell," Timmy says, taking in a deep breath of air through his nose.

I lift my head up and smell the air. "It smells like barbeque."

Timmy makes an educated guess. "Maybe Sir Licksalot followed the smell of the barbeque."

"If there is a barbeque, then that means there are people near by," Danny says, looking around hopefully.

Bobby starts walking. "Come on. If there are people they can help us find my sister."

Trying to catch up with Bobby, we sprint through the sugarcane along a trail. The sugarcane arches over the trail, smacking us in the face as we run through the muddy trail. Suddenly and without warning Timmy disappears. Desperately, the rest of us run to what appears to be the edge of a cliff and we slowly peek over the edge. We find ourselves looking down at a huge waterfall and there is a rainbow glowing in the mist over the water.

"Hello. I am dangling here!" Timmy calls out.

Something comes over me. I don't know what it is, but I have this sudden and incredible urge to touch the rainbow. I slowly take a few steps backwards, get a running start, and jump right through the rainbow.

When I surface in the pool below I see Timmy push off the ledge he is dangling from and he falls into the pool. Danny doesn't hesitate and he jumps right in too.

"I'm not missing this chance of a lifetime," Bobby shouts down to us. He takes a running start and jumps in, making the biggest splash of all of us.

Bobby surfaces and there is a huge smile on his face. "That was so sick!"

"Stay to the sides of the pool so the current doesn't pull us down the river," Danny tells us.

I look up and notice that the rainbow looks even more mesmerizing when you look up at it.

Then I remember something. "Didn't the book say that one of the Goddesses had her home in a place called Rainbow Falls?"

"Yep. Look for a cave behind the waterfall," Timmy says.

We swim behind the waterfall and to our surprise, we find a cave. We all climb out of the water to investigate.

"It's just like the book says," I say, looking at the walls.

"There are even pictures engraved in the rock, just like it says in the myth," says Bobby, with his eyes showing shock in them.

"Do you believe the myths now?" Danny asks.

Bobby is speechless as he rubs his fingers over the etchings on the rock. After investigating every detail of the cave, we sit down at the entrance and take it all in. Bobby adjusts his shorts. Danny places his hands on his cheeks, his elbows on his knees and expresses, "I can't believe we are here. Aloha!"

"Wait until Cici finds out what she missed," Bobby says.

Bobby is still fidgeting with his pockets while we sit captivated watching the water cascade down in front of us. Dark clouds start to form above us and the wind is picking up.

"Dude, what's up with the weather?" Timmy asks.

"Must be a tropical storm blowing in," Danny answers.

Moments later, Timmy says, "I really smell barbeque now. Can we go?"

"Absolutely! I want to make sure we find Cici and Sir Licksalot before it gets dark," I answer.

We dive back in and swim around to the other side of the pool where there is a narrow pathway. Danny makes sure we are still going in the correct direction with his GPS. "The river is on the left side so let's follow these natural stepping stones on the right until we reach the end."

CHAPTER 18
Hina's Wrath

The girls place the finished leis in the basket and walk a few hundred feet down to where the river meets the ocean. Cici is still reciting the mele, trying her best to perfect it.

Alana and Cici come to an area where there are lots of water-worn pebbles. "We will find your ili'ili' here," Alana tells Cici.

"How do I know which ones are the right ones?" Cici asks. "There are so many stones to choose from."

"Pick up two and place one against your palm holding it in place with your middle finger, ring finger and pinky finger. The other one is placed on top of it between your thumb and pointer finger. Like this," Alana shows Cici. "If the pebbles are too big, look for smaller ones. Tell me when you have found two that fit in each hand comfortably, then we will test the sound."

Cici begins her search. Out of the corner of her eye, Alana sees something moving nearby. She turns to see what it is. All she can see is something blackish with four legs. She quietly, yet quickly, gets Cici's attention whispering, "We have to leave right now!"

"Why?" Cici asks.

"Pua'a," Alana points.

Cici looks behind Alana. "That's not a pig. That is Sir Licksalot." Smacking her hands against her legs, Cici calls out. "Sir Licksalot, come over here boy!"

Sir Licksalot runs up to the girls licking Cici all over, tickling her as she giggles.

"My brother and the boys must be close by. This is Blaze's dog. Remember? I told you about him earlier."

Alana isn't paying close attention to what Cici is saying.

"Alana," Cici says looking up. Alana is stroking the cover of a book that has several tooth marks on it.

"Did you find your book?"

"No. He did," Alana replies, pointing to Sir Licksalot. Alana kneels down to Sir Licksalot and she hugs him. "Mahalo. Mahalo."

Cici continues her search for the ili'ili' while Alana makes friends with Sir Licksalot. The waves are crashing into the shore closer and closer to the girls and the sky is really dark as the wind whips their long hair around. After picking up dozens of pebbles, Cici finds the four that will fit in her hands perfectly. Walking back over to Alana and Sir Licksalot, she opens her hands and shows Alana her rocks. Alana shows Cici how to clap the pebbles together to make a rhythmic sound. Cici practices a few times and soon she is making pretty sounds. "Try to chant the mele while you are using the ili'ili'," Alana tells her.

The girls kneel down in a sandy area that is a little safer away from the crashing waves. "I'll go first and then you can join in," Alana suggests.

Cici agrees and follows Alana's lead to a tee. "You just preformed hula," Alana tells Cici after they have finished their practice.

"But I wasn't standing up. I thought you have to be standing up and moving your hips," Cici questions Alana.

"We will kneel for this one tonight. This hula is for the children," Alana explains. "It is sunset. We must go now."

"Okay. Can Sir Licksalot come to the luau?" Cici asks.

"Yes. We will honor him tonight. He will wear the red ohi'a lei," Alana says.

"The sacred flower?" Cici asks.

"Yes."

"But I thought you can't pick the ohi'a flower?" Cici says.

"A proper offering must be made first to Goddess Pele. We do this by making a lei at the top of the crater and tossing it into her pit. When we come down from Haleakala we can gather the flowers to wear without worrying about angering the goddess," Alana explains.

Cici nods her head in understanding as they make their way to the luau.

Bobby, Danny, Timmy, and I follow our noses, making our way along the narrow pathway. Up ahead we can see light and smoke from the flames on tiki torches.

Timmy rubs his stomach, "I sure hope they are cooking something good. I'm starving!"

After a sharp turn, we arrive in an open area where a group of people are enjoying a big party.

Timmy starts beat boxing:

> **Paapaa Partay**
> **Oh yeah,**
> **Oh yeah,**
> **Going to get some grub**
> **in my tub,**
> **Now who's the stud?!**

Still hidden behind the plants and trees we look around at all the people and their interesting costumes. I catch a glimpse of Sir Licksalot. I whistle and slap my leg, "Come here boy."

Sir Licksalot sprints over to us. He has a necklace of red flowers around his neck and he starts barking uncontrollably, jumping and running in circles.

"What is it boy?" I ask.

He trots away.

"Where is he going?" Timmy asks.

We don't move. We are frozen, afraid to intrude on the party.

Sir Licksalot finds Cici and barks at her.

"Dude, that's my sister. That's Cici," Bobby says, and he steps forward.

We slowly walk into the luau area and then four ladies step in front of us. Thinking we are in trouble for intruding, we stand still in silence.

"Aloha," the ladies say together. Then they place crowns of greenery on our heads. They point to our feet. Not sure what they want, I lift one leg up. One lady pulls my shoe off and she places a green leaf ring around my ankle. I remove my other shoe. Timmy, Danny, and Bobby remove theirs too. Before we know it, we are in costume.

Cici notices the commotion and she wanders over to see what is going on. A pretty Hawaiian girl follows her.

"Bobby, you made it just in time for the luau!" Cici squeals.

"Where have you been?" Bobby whispers.

"With my new best friend. Her name is Alana and she led me out of the forest," Cici explains. Cici introduces Alana and Bobby to each other.

Bobby can't speak. It is clear that he is smitten by Alana's beauty.

Cici continues the introductions, "These are my friends, Timmy, Danny, and the taller one is Blaze, Sir Licksalot's owner."

"Aloha," Alana greets us. "Please join us."

Feeling welcome, we relax and join the luau as sprinkles begin to fall on us from the dark clouds above. Alana's dad gets some burnt nut shell ash and with a smile on his face he paints some squiggly lines on our arms. He quickly finishes, nods, and then he returns to his people. We sit down facing everyone when a chant begins. Soon we hear the beat of clacking rocks and to our amazement we see that Cici is right in the middle of the group sitting next to Alana, chanting, and performing hula:

> **Mālama `o Hina i nā mea a pau loa mai luna mai**
> **o ka mahina**
> **Hō`omo`omo `o Pele i ka honua**
> **Ho`ohanohano `o Laka i nā mea a pau loa**
> **He mea ho`ākua nō kēia**
> **He mana nō ke aloha ā pilialoha**
> **Loa`a `ia i ka nani o Haleakalā**
> **I kēlā wahi wau i a`o `ia ai e pili ana ia'u**
> **Mai ka huaka`i i ke kai**

Just as they finish, Timmy pulls his coconut shells apart and whispers to us, "It's in da bag!" He begins a drum beat on the coconut shells and starts to chant:

> **Hawaii,**
> **The island of plenty**
> **Alana,**
> **Sweet as a pina colada**
> **Come on everybody,**
> **It's time to party**

Distracted by the food servers, Timmy looks over at the table mesmerized, still chanting and playing the coconut drums:

> **Yummy Poi**
> **Can't wait to enjoy**
> **Oh what a treat**
> **So much to eat**
> **Just don't sit next to Bobby's stinky feet**

Bobby pops Timmy in the back of the head, breaking his concentration. The luau guests clap for Timmy's effort.

Cici walks over to Bobby. "You were great. How did you know how to do that?" Bobby asks.

"Alana taught me. When I met her, she was picking the flowers for the leis. She showed me how to make the leis, sing the mele, and how to do the movements, but the best part was that she told me about the culture here in Hawaii and how respectful people should be. It feels so good to make people happy. I feel like I belong. I wish I could live here forever," Cici says.

"You will never believe where we have been. That book Sir Licksalot dug up…"

"The book is Alana's. She wrote it," Cici interrupts.

"The cave that is mentioned in the book is real Cici. We found it," Bobby divulges with excitement.

"What does it look like?" Cici asks.

Putting his hands in his pocket, Bobby pulls out a piece of the etched rock and shows Cici.

"You didn't take that from the cave, did you?" Cici inquires.

"I knew that you wouldn't believe me if I didn't show you," Bobby says.

"You have to put it back right away," Cici whispers.

"Why?" Bobby asks.

"Alana told me that if anything is disturbed in the cave we will witness Goddess Hina's wrath," Cici explains, looking worried.

Wondering what Cici and Bobby are whispering about, I interrupt. "What's up?"

"Bobby took a piece of rock from Hina's cave," Cici says.

"And? What does that mean?" Timmy asks.

"You don't want to find out. Go put it back Bobby. Hurry!"

Bobby runs up the steps back through the sugar cane while we wait, enjoying the local foods as the warm sprinkles begin to get heavier and colder.

Bobby makes his way back into the cave. He is trying to place the piece of rock that he took back inside the groove. Struggling to get it to fit properly, a piece chips off as he tries to forcefully push it in. Bobby wipes the sweat off his forehead and takes a deep breath. As he leaves the cave, the rain turns into a torrential down pour. The trees are swaying and twisting in the wind. Bobby hustles back down to the luau. Arriving at the luau area Bobby finds everyone trying to gather up the food to move to a dry location.

"Did you put it back?" Cici asks.

"Yes in the exact spot where I found it," Bobby says.

"The storm is Goddess Hina expressing her anger. You should not have disturbed the forest or anything in it. The cave is sacred to Goddess Hina. By removing a piece of it, you showed disrespect to the land," Alana explains.

"I don't see what the big deal is. It was just a piece of rock. I put it back." Bobby says, hiding the fact that he broke it trying to force it back into the groove.

Seemingly in response to these words, the rain gets even harder. Lighting strikes and thunder rolls across the sky. The ocean waves pound harder against the rocks.

"Bobby, be quiet. You are making things worse. She can hear us," Timmy says.

"Don't tell me you actually believe in all this baloney," Bobby says sarcastically.

Then Hina unleashes the full power of her anger on us.

"Run for cover! She is furious!" Alana screams.

Bobby starts apologizing. "I'm sorry. I'm sorry! I was just joking. I didn't mean to break it."

Frozen in place by our fear, none of us can move. Sir Licksalot is trembling. I pick up Sir Licksalot and tell the guys, "Let's find some cover."

Alana steps away from us so that she can retrieve her book. We battle the wind and the rain as we walk in single file holding on to each other's hands. Suddenly the water from a flash flood knocks us over, and we can no longer hold on to each other as we slide into the bubbling water of the three boiling pots. Still holding on to Sir Licksalot with a death grip, he and I get sucked under the water, and the rest of them soon follow us. Bobby and Cici are screaming, while Timmy and Danny flap their arms and kick their feet, trying to stay afloat. With little effort, the boiling pots suck us under and we are swirling around and around, going deeper and deeper.

CHAPTER 19
Aloha

Suddenly we surface, sliding down the waterfalls of the magical fountain. With an abrupt increase in water pressure we are shot out onto the lawn, landing on the grass in my backyard. Stunned to see that we are all alive, I lie on my back. I slowly turn my head to the side and I see that Sir Licksalot is chewing on his Dingo bone. Cici is pouting. Danny is checking his pockets to see if he has his gadgets. Timmy pulls out a tiny little fish from his shorts and Bobby is patting his arms and legs to make sure every part of him is still in one piece. I roll over and gradually sit up, a little dizzy from all the spinning around. It doesn't take long before Cici begins to attack Bobby. "Thanks Bobby for ruining my birthday celebration!"

"Me? You can't blame me for a storm," Bobby responds.

"Oh yes I can. As usual, you ruin everything," Cici says, glaring at her brother.

"That wasn't just any storm. That was a divine storm. That should prove to you that there is truth mixed in with the myths," Danny says.

"Yeah, well if that is true how come the Goddesses didn't show themselves earlier?" Bobby asks.

No one says anything as they contemplate Bobby's question.

Cici recalls what Alana told her. "Alana told me that the one who is in possession of her book is protected by the Goddesses. I can give you an example. When Alana had the book she didn't get swept into the boiling pots."

That jogged my memory. "When Sir Licksalot had the book he survived the muddy slope and he didn't get killed by the pigs."

"If Goddess Hina is supposed to protect children, why did she cause us to almost drown?" Bobby asks.

"I think she wanted to teach us a lesson about respect. She didn't want to kill us," I answer.

Bobby looks into the fountain noticing a few scared flowers floating and says, "Hmmm. Maybe you are right."

"Naturally," Timmy chimes in.

"Okay. I will respect the earth and other people. Happy?" Bobby says.

"It's about time," Timmy responds.

Walking away from the fountain, Bobby says, "The bottoms of my feet are killing me."

We all look down at our bare feet.

"Eh. I needed a new pair of shoes anyways," Bobby shares, and we all chuckle.

"We are still friends, right?" Bobby asks, looking worried.

I respond, "We couldn't be the Fools without you."

Bobby folds his fingers in and makes a fist, sticking his arm straight out horizontally. We all make a fist and gently touch knuckles, generating what the Hawaiians call mana.

Over Bobby's shoulder, I notice that Cici has a very happy expression on her face as she stares at the fountain.

"What's up Cici?" I ask.

"Think about it. This is only the third day of summer vacation and we have already visited Mavericks and Haleakala," Cici says, giving us a big grin.

Timmy's eyebrows rise in excitement. "And we are out of school for ten whole weeks. This summer vacation is going to rock!"

CPSIA information can be obtained at www.ICGtesting.com
Printed in the USA
LVOW050007140612

286009LV00001B/20/P